SCP

Secure. Contain. Protect.

Date: 25/10/█████████

Document security clearance level: Class D

Level 0 ☒   Level 1 ☐   Level 2 ☐   Level 3 ☐   Level 4 ☐

TABLE OF CONTENTS

CHAPTER 1 - ABOUT SCP BREAKOUT AND VGS

In this chapter we will brief you on your new job here with the Foundation as either a Player or a highly respected Game Master. We hope that our introduction documents will suffice as many personnel are busy at this time.

SCP Breakout is an SCP experience based on the large following of the horror genre of the same title. This game will allow you the player to enjoy and fear the life you lead here with the foundation. Through pen and paper RPG style gameplay tied in with dangerous SCP monsters, the experience is sure to lead to an everlasting experience! ... and possibly death (which we will not be held accountable for).

While the Game master will be able to make any scenarios they wish using this guidebook, there are included scenarios for your learning and instructional experience at the end of this book. Specifically this book focuses on the worst case scenario at a Facility; a massive breakout of SCP. This situation is dangerous and rare, but everyone must understand what to do in such a situation.

Breakout training information and procedure can be found at **[REDACTED]**.

NOTE: VGS (or Versatility Gaming System) is the title for the gaming system SCP Breakout uses. It is a new and immersive system focusing on storytelling over dice rolls for a fast paced and intense experience. This system has been adapted for use specifically with SCP Breakout and can not be promised to be compatible with another system or game.

SCP

Secure. Contain. Protect.

Date: 25/10/██████

Document security clearance level: Class C

Level 0 ☐   Level 1 ☑   Level 2 ☐   Level 3 ☐   Level 4 ☐

CHAPTER 2 - CREATING A CHARACTER

In this chapter we will take a psycho analysis of yourself. We need to be fully assured that you will be able to follow rules and protocols in the Foundation. A lot of the things you will see here will be beyond normal human comprehension and will require a stable and adaptive mind to resist breakdowns.

We will break down your psycho analysis into the following steps:

1. Reviewing your gender, height, weight, and necessary physical details
2. Determining your Class in the Foundation
3. Determining your Position in the Foundation
4. Discovering Special Skills you may possess
5. Discovering any special Feats and Flaws
6. List any Equipment you possess or require upon entering the Foundation

STEP 1 - PHYSICAL DETAILS

Firstly grab a Psycho Analysis sheet from the back of the document. This can be done via printing, scanning, or removing the sheet. More sheets are available online if required.

The sheet contains locations for Player name where your name will go, GM where your game masters name will go, sections for height, weight, eye color, and hair color of your character. These can all be filled out on your whims desire, express yourself in any way you see fit here.

The sheet also contains an area for HP, AV, and Sanity. These physical traits will be given based on your position and class in the foundation in later steps.

STEP 2 - DETERMINING YOUR CLASS

The foundation follows a very strict Class system ranging from A-E. Classifications are assigned to personnel based on their proximity to potentially dangerous anomalous objects, entities, or phenomena. They are described as follows:

CLASS A

Class A personnel are those deemed essential to Foundation strategic operations, and are not allowed direct access to anomalies under any circumstances. When circumstances require Class A personnel to be in direct proximity to such anomalies (such as in the case of facilities housing containment units), Class A personnel are not allowed access to the areas of the facility containing such anomalies and are to be kept in secured areas at all times.

Date: 25/10/███████

Document security clearance level: Class C

Level 0 ☐   Level 1 ☑   Level 2 ☐   Level 3 ☐   Level 4 ☐

In the case of an emergency, Class A personnel are to be immediately evacuated to a designated and secure off-site location. O5 Council members are always Class A personnel.

This Class should be reserved for NPC's and important plot characters as it would rarely be seen in a normal game.

CLASS B

Class B personnel are those deemed essential to local Foundation operations, and may only be granted access to objects, entities, and anomalies that have passed quarantine and have been cleared of any potential mind-affecting effects or mimetic agents. In the event of a containment breach or hostile action against a Foundation facility, Class B personnel are to be evacuated to a designated, secure off-site location as soon as possible.

This Class is not recommended for play because of their overly extreme safeguarding procedures. However a Class B caught up working with Class D's in a catastrophic breakdown of a facility could be very entertaining.

CLASS C

Class C personnel are personnel with direct access to most anomalies not deemed strictly hostile or dangerous. Class C personnel that have had direct contact with potentially mind-affecting or mimetic properties may be subject to mandatory quarantine and psychiatric evaluation as deemed necessary by security personnel. In the event of a containment breach or hostile action against a Foundation facility, non-combatant Class C personnel are to either report to secure lock-down areas or evacuated at the discretion of on-site security personnel in the case of a site-wide breach or other catastrophic event.

Class C's can be quite fun to play as they are exposed to main parts of the facility, but do not ever come into direct contact with hostile SCP. This makes playing them in a breakout very nerve wrecking as they would have knowledge of the SCP they encounter knowing just how hostile the threat is they are facing.

SCP

Secure. Contain. Protect.

Date: 25/10/███████

Document security clearance level: Class C

Level 0 ☐   Level 1 ☒   Level 2 ☐   Level 3 ☐   Level 4 ☐

CLASS D

Class D personnel are expendable personnel used to handle extremely hazardous anomalies and are not allowed to come into contact with Class A or Class B personnel. Class D personnel are typically drawn worldwide from the ranks of prison inmates convicted of violent crimes, especially those on death row. In times of duress, Protocol 12 may be enacted, which allows recruitment from other sources — such as political prisoners, refugee populations, and other civilian sources — that can be transferred into Foundation custody under plausibly deniable circumstances. Class D personnel are to be given regular mandatory psychiatric evaluations and are to be administered an amnesic of at least Class B strength or terminated at the end of the month at the discretion of on-site security or medical staff. In the event of a catastrophic site event, Class D personnel are to be terminated immediately except as deemed necessary by on-site security personnel.

This is exactly why Class D are the most entertaining to play. They have no reason not to try and take their freedom during a breakout, and have no allies besides other class D personnel, and potentially some Class C who have worked with them. They are also usually stronger and understand violence more due to their criminal nature.

CLASS E

Class E is a provisional classification applied to field agents and containment personnel that have been exposed to potentially dangerous effects during the course of securing and establishing initial containment over a newly-designated anomalous object, entity, or phenomenon. Class E personnel are to be quarantined as soon as possible, monitored, and screened for potentially harmful changes in behavior, personality, or physiology, and may only return to duty after being fully debriefed and cleared by psychiatric and medical staff.

Class E players are hard to work in unless they are found in containment during the time of the breakdown of a facility. In this way they can be introduced to the group, and in fact have some adverse effects from whatever SCP they had worked with before their quarantine.

While the best games are played with only Class D, and possible Class E players, we included all classes so that you could potentially use them in your game. The Class you pick while not having direct stat changes, will affect how you can play, and what Specialties and Faults you can take.

Once you've decided on your class you may fill it in on your Psycho Analysis sheet.

Secure. Contain. Protect.

Date: 25/10/ ████████

Document security clearance level: Class C

Level 0 ☐   Level 1 ☒   Level 2 ☐   Level 3 ☐   Level 4 ☐

STEP 3 - POSITION IN THE FOUNDATION

Your position for our foundation will be the pinnacle of your success and contribution to the safety of the world. While many classes of personnel are able to choose their positions, there are a few who must play their part for the greater good of everyone and everything.

These positions are lengthy in description, will determine some of your stats and will influence what you will have access to in the Foundation. As such you will have to pardon our asking that you take the time to read CHAPTER 3 before choosing your position. In SCP Breakout, you will only be allowed to choose ONE position, so please take your time and choose carefully. Crossing positional roles in our containment structure could lead to **[REDACTED]** and therefore is not allowed.

Once you have decided on your Position you may enter it on your Psycho Analysis sheet under Position. You may then proceed to calculate your HP, Sanity, and Position Bonuses.

STEP 4 - SKILL ALLOCATION

This step is one of the most important and will influence your ability to perform tasks throughout the foundation. On your sheet you have various skills, these are a measure of your prowess physically and mentally. All of your skills start at 10. You may then move points between skills, for instance taking 2 points from Strength and putting them into smarts would make strength 8 (10-2) and smarts 12 (10+2).

The skill system goes off the premise that the higher your skill value is, the worse you are at that skill. In order to succeed in a skill you must roll higher than it's value. So if a skill is 5, then on a D20 you must roll higher than 5 to succeed. In this way rolls are fast and easy to do at a glance, the smaller your skill value, the better you are.

The GM can choose what the max and minimum values are for moving points. We recommend the following based on the difficulty the GM wishes the game to be.

Easy = 4 (min) and 16 (max), Normal = 6 (min) and 14 (max), Hard = 8 (min) and 12 (max), Very Hard = They can only move 4 points in total.

Skills will be more greatly defined in CHAPTER 4, with uses, bonuses, and skill saves.

SCP

Secure. Contain. Protect.

Date: 25/10/ ████

Document security clearance level: Class C

Level 0 ☐   Level 1 ☒   Level 2 ☐   Level 3 ☐   Level 4 ☐

STEP 5 - FEATS AND FLAWS

This step is for the specialist out there. While everyone has feats and flaws, some people have more than others. These can be things like scaring easily, being more resistant to pain, being more athletic, having bad eyesight, and much more.

Feats and flaws are described in CHAPTER 5, and have restrictions based on position and class.

Feats and flaws can be written under feats and flaws sections of your Psycho Analysis sheet. All players must have equal points in feats and flaws. If a player has 2pts in flaws, then they can have 2pts in feats; while a player with 4pts in feats cannot have less than 4pts in flaws.

STEP 6 - EQUIPMENT

Equipment is rarely allowed to be brought into the foundation sites, but some exceptions are allowed for higher level personnel. We however do not permit any equipment to ever be taken off site. Each Position has it's own standard equipment in which new members such as yourself are given upon entry into our Foundation. If your require more equipment special requests may be made from our Equipment list in CHAPTER 6, and must be approved by a CLASS B or higher personnel or your GM.

Date: 25/10/█████

Document security clearance level: Class D

Level 0 ☒   Level 1 ☐   Level 2 ☐   Level 3 ☐   Level 4 ☐

CHAPTER 3 - FOUNDATION POSITIONS

In this chapter we will assessing your future role in the Foundation! We are happy to have you and as our classification system has determined you may be eligible for multiple positions here (or none depending).

CLASS A POSITIONS:

These positions are not usually available to players unless the GM has a specific reason to do so. These are the most important members of the entire foundation and will not usually ever come into contact with any SCP directly. In fact they generally only go to facilities on very routines runs for data and progress / containment reports.

SITE DIRECTOR

Site directors for major Foundation facilities are the highest-ranking personnel at that location and are responsible for the continued, safe operation of the site and all of its contained anomalies and projects. All major departmental directors report directly to the Site Director, who in turn reports to the O5 Council.

HEALTH: 34, SANITY: 20, ARMOR: 6

ADJ: +2 Might, +1 Agility, -1 Smarts,
     -2 Influence

	HEAD	BODY	ARMS	LEGS
HEALTH	4	10	5/5	5/5
ARMOR	0	4	1/1	0/0

O5 COUNCIL MEMBER

The O5 Council refers to the committee consisting of the highest-ranking directors of the Foundation. With complete access to all information regarding anomalies in containment, the O5 Council oversees all Foundation operations worldwide and directs its long-term strategic plans. Due to the sensitivity of their positions, O5 Council members must not come into direct contact with any anomalous object, entity, or phenomenon. Furthermore, the identities of all O5 Council members is classified; all council members are referred to only by their numeric designation (O5-1 through O5-13).

O5 Council Members are not playable.

SCP

Secure. Contain. Protect.

Date: 25/10/ ██████

Document security clearance level: Class D

Level 0 ☒ Level 1 ☐ Level 2 ☐ Level 3 ☐ Level 4 ☐

CLASS B POSITIONS:

Class B positions are again not recommended for players as they are usually evacuated immediately after a breach in security. The few class B's that do stay are the Security teams meant to capture and contain Class D, Class E and SCP hostiles.

CONTAINMENT SPECIALIST

Containment specialists have two main roles at Foundation facilities. Firstly, containment teams are called upon to respond to confirmed cases of anomalous activity to secure and establish initial containment over anomalous objects, entities, or phenomena and transport them to the nearest Foundation containment site. In addition, Foundation containment engineers and technicians are called upon to devise, refine, and maintain containment units and schemes for objects, entities, and phenomena in Foundation facilities.

HEALTH: 52, SANITY: 30, ARMOR: 14

ADJ: +1 Might, +1 Influence,
    -1 Smarts, -1 Experience

	HEAD	BODY	ARMS	LEGS
HEALTH	5	15	8/8	8/8
ARMOR	1	7	2/2	1/1

TACTICAL RESPONSE OFFICER

Response teams — or tactical teams — are highly trained and heavily armed combat teams tasked with escorting containment teams when dangerous anomalous entities or hostile Groups of Interest are involved and defending Foundation facilities against hostile action. Response teams are effectively military units stationed at major Foundation facilities that are ready to deploy at a moment's notice.

HEALTH: 65, SANITY: 35, ARMOR: 35

ADJ: +1 Smarts, +3 Influence,
    -2 Might, -1 Vitality, -1 Agility

	HEAD	BODY	ARMS	LEGS
HEALTH	6	19	10/10	10/10
ARMOR	5	10	5/5	5/5

SCP

Secure. Contain. Protect.

Date: 25/10/▓▓▓▓

Document security clearance level: Class D

Level 0 ☒   Level 1 ☐   Level 2 ☐   Level 3 ☐   Level 4 ☐

CLASS C POSITIONS:

Class C positions are great positions for players as they interact with the anomalies and work with the Class D's (well technically watch over them). While class D's are probably the most fun as they have reason to escape the Facilities, Class C personnel would be able to identify and understand the danger of the SCP's that they would encounter.

RESEARCHER

Researchers are the scientific branch of the Foundation, drawn from the ranks of the smartest and best-trained research scientists from around the world. With specialists in every field imaginable, from chemistry and botany to more esoteric or specialized fields such as theoretical physics and xenobiology, the goal of the Foundation's research projects is to gain a better understanding of unexplained anomalies and how they operate.

HEALTH: 28, *SANITY:* 50, *ARMOR:* 7

ADJ: +2 Might, +1 Influence,
      +1 Agility, -2 Smarts,
      -2 Experience

	HEAD	BODY	ARMS	LEGS
HEALTH	4	10	4/4	3/3
ARMOR	0	1	1/1	0/0

SECURITY OFFICER

On-site security officers — often referred to simply as guards — at Foundation facilities are tasked with maintaining physical and information security for Foundation projects, operations, and personnel. Primarily drawn and recruited from military, law enforcement, and correctional facility personnel, security officers are trained in the use of all types of weapons as well as a variety of contingency plans covering both containment breach incidents as well as hostile action. These personnel are also responsible for information security, such as making sure that sensitive documents are not misplaced and that a facility's computer systems are safe from outside intrusion. They are also often the first line of defense against hostile outside forces for Foundation facilities.

HEALTH: 39, *SANITY:* 30, *ARMOR:* 30

ADJ: +1 Smarts, +2 Influence,
      -1 Might, -1 Vitality,
      -1 Experience

	HEAD	BODY	ARMS	LEGS
HEALTH	4	15	5/5	5/5
ARMOR	0	10	5/5	5/5

SCP

Secure. Contain. Protect.

Date: 25/10/▐▐▐▐▐

Document security clearance level: Class D

Level 0 ☒   Level 1 ☐   Level 2 ☐   Level 3 ☐   Level 4 ☐

CLASS D POSITIONS:

Class D personnel are expendable personnel used to handle extremely hazardous anomalies and are not allowed to come into contact with Class A or Class B personnel. Class D personnel are typically drawn worldwide from the ranks of prison inmates convicted of violent crimes, especially those on death row. In times of duress, Protocol 12 may be enacted, which allows recruitment from other sources — such as political prisoners, refugee populations, and other civilian sources — that can be transferred into Foundation custody under plausibly deniable circumstances. Class D personnel are to be given regular mandatory psychiatric evaluations and are to be administered an amnesiac of at least Class B strength or terminated at the end of the month at the discretion of on-site security or medical staff. In the event of a catastrophic site event, Class D personnel are to be terminated immediately except as deemed necessary by on-site security personnel.

This is exactly why Class D are the most entertaining to play. They have no reason not to try and take their freedom during a breakout, and have no allies besides other class D personnel, and potentially some Class C who have worked with them.

CLASS D

Class D personnel are simply Class D's. When brought into the facility they already were on death row and had lost their rights, now they are basically just guinea pigs for the researchers. Class D's are always clearly marked with a barcode tattoo somewhere on their person as well as an orange jumpsuit, similar to a prison garb. They are rarely allowed around the facility without armed guards watching them.

HEALTH: 35, SANITY: 40, ARMOR: 0

ADJ: +2 Experience, +1 Influence,
    -1 Agility, -2 Might

	HEAD	BODY	ARMS	LEGS
HEALTH	5	10	5/5	5/5
ARMOR	0	0	0/0	0/0

Date: 25/10/▮▮▮▮▮

Document security clearance level: Class D

Level 0 ☒ Level 1 ☐ Level 2 ☐ Level 3 ☐ Level 4 ☐

CLASS E POSITIONS:

Class E is a provisional classification applied to field agents and containment personnel that have been exposed to potentially dangerous effects during the course of securing and establishing initial containment over a newly-designated anomalous object, entity, or phenomenon. Class E personnel are to be quarantined as soon as possible, monitored, and screened for potentially harmful changes in behavior, personality, or physiology, and may only return to duty after being fully debriefed and cleared by psychiatric and medical staff.

Class E players are hard to work in unless they are found in containment during the time of the breakdown of a facility. In this way they can be introduced to the group, and in fact have some adverse effects from whatever SCP they had worked with before their quarantine.

FIELD AGENT

Field agents are the eyes and ears of the Foundation, personnel trained to look for and investigate signs of anomalous activity, often undercover with local or regional law enforcement or embedded in local services such as emergency medical services and regulatory organizations. As undercover units, field agents are typically not equipped to deal with confirmed cases of anomalous activity; once such an incident has been confirmed and isolated, field agents will typically call for assistance from the nearest field containment team with the means to safely secure and contain such anomalies.

HEALTH: 45, SANITY: 35, ARMOR: 20

ADJ: +2 Vitality, +1 Agility,
     -1 Might, -2 Smarts

	HEAD	BODY	ARMS	LEGS
HEALTH	10	15	5/5	5/5
ARMOR	5	5	3/3	2/2

Secure. Contain. Protect.

Date: 25/10/████

Document security clearance level: Class C

Level 0 ☐   Level 1 ☒   Level 2 ☐   Level 3 ☐   Level 4 ☐

CHAPTER 4 - SKILLS

As a valuable member of the Foundation you will be required to perform many tasks around our facilities. These require that you be assessed on your prowess in various different skills. As previously stated all of your skill values start at 10, denoting the average worker. You may then take points out of one skill and put them into another. For example taking 3 Points out of Might and putting 2 into Smarts and 1 into Experience. This would result in Might being 7 (10-3), Smarts being 12 (10+2), and Experience being 11 (10+1).

In the VGS system that our forms use, a lower value in your skills is superior. This is because performing a task requires you to roll 1D20 to try and beat your skill value. Using the stats presented earlier in this chapter, rolling for Might would be easier than rolling for Smarts. This is because rolling higher than 7 on a D20 is easier than rolling higher than a 12 on a D20.

Having a tie on a skill check should be met with a second roll. The GM should then take the opportunity to work in a situation that is not favorable where the player rarely scrapes by or just fails, based on their second roll.

Most Player Characters should not be allowed to have any skills start below 5 or above 15. This prevents godly or strangely overpowered humans. Also we will know you are lying on your evaluation which will result in **[REDACTED]**.

SKILL DEFINITIONS:

Our skills are very defined in what they represent, and what they will tell us about you. For your own knowledge we will present you with the basics of our skill system to help you self assess your own abilities for your form.

<u>MIGHT</u>

Might is the definition of your physical strength. This encompasses your ability to lift, push, and punch things. Might also gives us here at the foundation a baseline for your physical fighting prowess for **[REDACTED]**. Might has other benefits detailed in CHAPTER 5 - FEATS & FLAWS, attached.

MIGHT	0-1	2-4	5-8	9-11	12-15	15-19	20+
Lift Weight	400+ lbs	250 lbs	170 lbs	110 lbs	70 lbs	50 lbs	30 lbs
Melee DMG	+5	+3	+1	0	-1	-3	-5

Date: 25/10/█████████

Document security clearance level: Class C

Level 0 ☐   Level 1 ☒   Level 2 ☐   Level 3 ☐   Level 4 ☐

AGILITY

Agility is your physical ability to run, jump, balance, dodge, and sneak around. It is a versatile skill that we would expect all subjects to have in some regard. Agility is especially useful when trying to **[REDACTED]** from **[REDACTED]**. Benefits of good agility can be found in CHAPTER 5 - FEATS & FLAWS, attached.

VITALITY

Vitality is your physical endurance, and health. It's the idealization of your physical survival aspects. This could include surviving physical strain and punishment, resisting diseases and poisons, avoiding bleeding out or losing consciousness, or even **[REDACTED]**. Benefits to good health have physical benefits detailed in CHAPTER 5 - FEATS & FLAWS, attached.

SMARTS

Smarts is the value of your mental prowess and problem solving. Smarts more specifically involves your ability to think on the spot, solve scientific and medical problems, like when **[REDACTED]** happened in case # **[REDACTED]**. It does not encompass general knowledge or experience. Benefits to a gifted mind are detailed in CHAPTER 5 - FEATS & FLAWS, attached.

EXPERIENCE

Experience is the culmination of your mental and physical knowledge. It covers experience with work, social skills, and of course with the Foundation. The longer you have worked here the more experience you will have, meaning more knowledge of SCP's and the foundations information. All this experience is confidential and will be wiped from the memories of all Class D personnel upon release by **[REDACTED]**. There are more benefits for experienced foundation members in CHAPTER 5 - FEATS & FLAWS, attached.

INFLUENCE

Influence is the social aptitude of your being. It is the ability for you to talk your way out of a situation, charm someone, intimidate them, or rally others. This skill is often used to handle social anomalies or situations where **[REDACTED]** is necessary. There are many more benefits to being influential in the foundation. These can be found in CHAPTER 5 - FEATS & FLAWS, attached.

Date: 25/10/███████

Document security clearance level: Class B

Level 0 ☐   Level 1 ☐   Level 2 ⊠   Level 3 ☐   Level 4 ☐

CHAPTER 5 - FEATS AND FLAWS

In this chapter we will analyze your useful skills that we classify as "feats" that will help the foundation and your work. The skills we find in detriment to your usefulness will be deemed as "flaws" and will count against your position here. We make sure that all 'employees' chosen for the Foundation have at least 2 more "points" in designated Feats than they do in flaws.

As such all evaluation forms should start with 2 feat points to spend. All other points can be earned by writing down flaws to get more feats. For example a form with 3 points in flaws can take 5 points in feats (2 initial points plus 3 from the flaws).

Our Feats are listed alphabetically, followed by our acknowledged flaws. Please go through and fill out your form as necessary before moving onto the next chapter.

FEATS

ACCURATE
[Vitality below 7] (2pt)
After years of watching your back and gunfighting or hunting you have become very accurate in your sight. As you look around you notice details other people don't set eyes on. This level of perception gives you +2 on rolls to spot or find things visually, and +1 to attack rolls with a ranged weapon.

ACROBATIC
[Agility below 8] (2pt)
Acrobatics is a feat showing expertise in climbing and balancing. This feat gives you +2 to climbing and balance checks, as well as the ability to take checks on what should be impossible climbs or impossible balance checks.

ALERTNESS
[Experience below 8] (2pt)
Alert characters have had experience being surprised and caught off guard, and are more aware because of it. This has resulted in them being more attuned and reactive to danger. These characters get +2 to initiative rolls, and can make an "Alertness" roll to avoid surprises.

NOTE: Feats and flaws can also add additional skills the employee can perform. Update when possible.

- EID: 4587

Date: 25/10/█████

Document security clearance level: Class B

Level 0 ☐   Level 1 ☐   Level 2 ☒   Level 3 ☐   Level 4 ☐

ANATOMY
[Experience below 9] (2-4pt)
Characters with Anatomy understand the workings of the human body. For 4 points you can have knowledge of SCP Anatomy as determined by the GM. This allows you to perform critical hits against these targets on a 19-20 instead of just a 20.

ANIMAL EMPATHY
[Influence below 8] (1pt)
Characters with animal empathy are able to more easily calm, manipulate, and befriend animals, or animal like SCP. They get +1 to checks to influence or ride an animal.

APPRAISE ITEM
[Smarts below 7] (2pt)
Characters who can appraise items in SCP are invaluable. We are not talking item values as most things in SCP and invaluable, but you are skill enough to appraise their usefulness. You can determine simple uses or effects of an item after a few minutes of inspection and a successful smarts check.

ARMOR MASTER
[Might below 7, Armor Work Feat] (3pt)
You are a master of armor, you understand that each piece is important and how they fit is a masterwork of their design. As such you get +2 to each armor location, and you ignore 3 points of armor when attacking.

ARMOR WORK
[Might below 8] (2pt)
You are a purveyor of armor, you understand that each piece is important and how they fit is a masterwork of their design. As such you get +1 to each armor location, and you ignore 1 point of armor when attacking.

ATTRACTIVE
[None] (1-5pt)
You are more lovely than usual when viewed by anyone who would be attracted to your gender. For 1pt your character is attractive and gets +1 to influence others who would be attracted to you. For 3pts your character is very attractive (like a supermodel) and gets +2 to influence others who would be attracted to you. For 5pts your character is more attractive than should be possible and gets +3 to influence others who would be attracted to you.

BACKSTAB
[Agility below 7, Sneaky Feat] (2pt)
Backstabbers are skilled at sneaking up on people and getting them from behind. As such when surprising a target in combat or attacking from behind you do +1D damage that ignores armor.

BLIND FIGHTING
[Accurate Feat, Acrobatic Feat] (2pt)
You are able to perfectly fight in conditions where you cannot see, or choose to close your eyes. Blinding effects or no visibility does not affect your combat rolls.

SCP

Secure. Contain. Protect.

Date: 25/10/█████████

Document security clearance level: Class B

Level 0 ☐   Level 1 ☐   Level 2 ☒   Level 3 ☐   Level 4 ☐

BRAVADO
[Might Below 8] (1pt)
You are rash in combat, refusing to show weakness by falling back from your enemies' blows. You may not gain the benefit of any kind of dodge bonuses or be able to flee from a combat. However your bravery is over the top and as such you get +4 to rolls against fear or loss of sanity.

BREATHING EXPERT
[Vitality Below 8] (2pt)
You are a skilled breather and have practiced breathing techniques for years. This has resulted in you being able to control your breathing excellently, and causes you to be able to last twice as long in dangerous breathing environments or underwater. You can also take 10min to reduce your stress level by 1 with deep breathing (This cannot reduce your stress level below 1).

CHASTE
[None] (1pt)
Your character does not have a sexual drive, or has suppressed it immeasurably. As such they cannot be charmed or sexually attracted to any gender or SCP that influences charm.

CHOKE HOLD
[Might Below 9, Agility Below 9, Unarmed Combat training Feat, Grappler] (1pt)
Your character knows how to hold someone in the correct way to render them unconscious. If you successfully grapple an opponent you may then make a choke hold Might check. If you pass the character is rendered unconscious for 2D4 rounds.

If you continue the choke hold for 2 additional rounds they will die.

COMPUTER HACKER
[Smarts Below 6, Computer Wiz] (2pt)
Characters with this skill can use and program computers with expert skill. They can gather information or access middle to high level encoded files on any computational device.

COMPUTER WIZ
[Smarts Below 8, Computer Wiz] (2pt)
Characters with this skill can use and program computers with intermediate skill. They can gather information or access low level encoded files on any computational device.

COORDINATED ATTACK
[Smarts Below 9, Another Player with this Feat] (2pt)
You and another player with this feat are very coordinated in combat. When you both attack the same target you can both make 2 attacks instead of 1.

COUNTER ATTACK
[Agility Below 8] (2pt)
Whenever an opponent attacks and misses they leave a window for you to exploit. Every time an opponent makes an attack against you that is unsuccessful, you may make an attack of opportunity against them (As long as you have the tools/weapons to do so).

Date: 25/10/███████

Document security clearance level: Class B

Level 0 ☐   Level 1 ☐   Level 2 ☒   Level 3 ☐   Level 4 ☐

DAUNTING PRESENCE
[Influence Below 7] (2pt)
You are a terrifying individual. You get +2 on influence rolls to intimidate, and can cause fear on your intimidations when you critical.

DECEITFUL
[Influence Below 9] (1pt)
You are very very good at lying to others, including your friends. You get +2 to rolls to deceive others, as well as +1 to smarts to catch someone else speaking lies to you.

DEFLECTION (EXPERT)
[Agility Below 6, Deflection (Novice) Feat] (2pt)
You are amazingly fast when it comes to projectiles, being able to swat them out of the air. As such you can make a Agility roll at -2 to deflect arrows and thrown objects out of the air once per round.

DEFLECTION (NOVICE)
[Agility Below 8] (2pt)
Either through luck or amazingly impossible skill you can deflect physical blows against you. As such you can make Agility rolls in melee combat to deflect a successful blow once per round.

DEFT HANDS
[Agility Below 9] (1pt)
You may perform checks that involve performing a hand action in plain sight silently or hidden. An example would be your ability to pickpocket someone who is awake, or to pull a gun / knife out in front of someone without their knowledge, or to hide something on your person quickly within sight of your victim.

These are known as "Sleight of Hand" checks, and use your Agility.

DIE HARD
[Vitality Below 7, Health Nut (2+) Feat] (2pt)
You don't go down easily, and will fight even when on deaths door. As such when you are out of HP you may continue to fight or move in a round, but not both. Your movement is also halved, and damage is halved. You will die if your HP goes to -10.

ENDURANCE TRAINING
[Agility Below 9 or Might Below 9 or Vitality Below 9] (3pt)
Your character is great at performing physical tasks over long periods of time without strain to their body. As such when moving up the strain track you only move up half (moving 1 up the strain track does not affect you).

ENGINEERING KNOWLEDGE
[Smarts Below 8] (2pt)
Your character is very machine smart. As such they can dismantle and fix almost anything. They do +1 damage to machine enemies, ignore armor on machine enemies, and can make smarts checks to fix machines and vehicles of all kinds. They can attempt to use these skills on mechanical SCP at a -4.

Date: 25/10/▮▮▮▮

Document security clearance level: Class B

Level 0 ☐   Level 1 ☐   Level 2 ☒   Level 3 ☐   Level 4 ☐

ETHEREAL CONNECTION
[None] (2pt)
You have the ability to see spirits and other paranormal SCP, as well as make a sense Paranormal check once every hour. This check for SCP also tells you how hostile their energy is. The GM must tell you if the SCP you sense is friendly, neutral, or hostile.

EXTREME CONDITIONAL TRAINING
[Vitality Below 6, Survival Training Feat] (3pt)
You know how to live in the worst harsh conditions possible. You get +4 to your checks to navigate, as well as for food and water searches. You can also use your check to determine dangerous gases in the air, plants, or animals. This check can be taken against SCP to determine it's disposition as friendly, neutral, or hostile at a -4.

FEARLESS
[Experience Below 8] (2pt)
Your character believes they are fearless. Nothing scares them anymore, at least until they came to the foundation. SCP are terrifying, and as such can still cause you to be afraid, however all fear done to you is halved when moving up the fear track. Moving 1 up the fear track does not affect you as it is not scary enough.

FEIGN INJURY
[Experience Below 8, Influence Below 9] (1pt)
Your good at faking injuries to throw off attackers. A successful influence check to fake an injury will cause enemies to believe you to be an easy target. Any attacker failing an experience save will open themselves up to an attack of opportunity on their next attack against you. You can only fool each enemy once with this tactic.

FIGHT OR FLIGHT INSTINCT
[Experience Below 9, Vitality Below 9] (2pt)
Your character has a very thorough fight or flight mechanic. As such your character can make a experience roll when a hostile force is near (either living like an enemy, or non living like a automated trap), to know that something is wrong. When face to face with something they are unsure about, they can once a day make a vitality check to have the GM tell them if their instinct says to fight or run away.

FLEXIBLE
[Agility Below 8] (2pt)
Being Flexible you are able to fit into areas ¼ your size (uncomfortably), you can also perform the escape artist check using agility to get out of bonds, cages, or other traps.

GOOD KARMA
[Influence Below 9, or Experience below 9] (3pt)
Your character has always had good luck and a good life. Besides being wrongly accused and put on death row their life had been perfect. As such karma is trying it's best to pay you back and you get double karma when you earn karma points, as well as half curse points (gaining 1 curse point will not affect you).

SCP

Date: 25/10/█████

Document security clearance level: Class B

Level 0 ☐   Level 1 ☐   Level 2 ☒   Level 3 ☐   Level 4 ☐

GRAPPLER
[Might Below 7, Unarmed Combat Training Feat] (2pt)
Your character is good at manipulating combat and holding opponents. As such with a Might check against an opponents might you can grapple them, causing them to be unable to move or attack until they pass a Might check to escape. You can melee them while they are held, but they can defend themselves without dodging. Options after a successful grapple are to hold, throw 5ft, or attack. Throwing 5ft leaves the victim prone.

HARD FIST
[Might Below 7] (1pt)
Your character has stone hard punches. They can break through some wooden objects by punching and get +2 on unarmed melee damage.

HEALTH NUT
[Vitality Below 9] (1-3pt)
Your character is healthier than normal, for each point of Health Nut you take (up to 3) add 1HP to each of your body parts (head, Body, each arm, and each leg).

HIGH SOCIETY
[Influence Below 9] (1pt)
You are used to talking with higher ups, rich and classy persons, and so forth. As such you get +2 to influence rolls when talking with "classy" or Class B-A persons / SCP.

IRON GUT
[Vitality below 8] (1pt)
Your stomach is amazingly good at filtering out bad contaminants. If you eat something diseased or poisoned you resist it. If you eat something from an SCP you get a 50% chance to resist it's effect.

LACERATE
[Experience Below 7, Backstab Feat, Anatomy Feat] (2pt)
Lacerate means that you have a knowledge of the arteries on the target, either through previous experience or medical knowledge. With Lacerate you cause all targets you hit with a piercing or slashing weapon to bleed for 1D4 damage a round.

MULTIATTACK
[Unarmed Combat Feat] (2pt)
You are fast on your feet and even faster when fighting unarmed. This feat allows you to take an additional unarmed attack in combat.

MULTIWEAPON FIGHTING
[Weapon Mastery (Any Melee)] (2pt)
You are skilled with both hands wielding weapons. You can use this skill to either make two melee weapon attacks in a combat turn, or fire a one handed ranged weapon and make a one handed melee attack in the same combat turn.

NATURAL HEALING
[Vitality Below 6] (2pt)
You seem to have a tough and restorative body. While outside of combat you regenerate 1 Health point per 10min, up to 3/4 your maximum health.

SCP

Secure. Contain. Protect.

Date: 25/10/█████

Document security clearance level: Class B

Level 0 ☐   Level 1 ☐   Level 2 ☒   Level 3 ☐   Level 4 ☐

NEGOTIATOR
[Influence Below 9] (1pt)
Your character is great at changes other demeanor toward you. As such you may make a Attitude Check (using Influence) to determine someones stance toward you, and make them 1 level friendlier.

NIGHT VISION
[Agility Below 9] (1pt)
Your character can see normally in low light, and half their normal sight range in pitch darkness.

NIMBLE FINGERS
[Agility Below 9] (1pt)
You have fast small fingers that allow you to work with delicate devices. You can analyze and disable devices and traps with +2 to agility.

NORMALIZED MENTAL STATE
[Smarts Below 6] (2pt)
Your mind is a fortress, and a miracle, able to sort through terrifying situations quickly and repair damage done. While outside any fear or mental strain (including combat) you regenerate 1 Sanity point per 5min.

PLAN B
[Smarts Below 9, Experience Below 8] (2pt)
You always have a plan in case plan A fails, as such you can once per session say you have a Plan B and describe it. If you can do so you can reroll a failed check or set of checks (determined by the GM) that were part of your "Plan A".

PLAYING POSSUM
[Influence Below 8] (1pt)
You are good at faking defenselessness or death. As such you get +4 to your influence to fake your death or appear defenseless. SCP and animals that use other senses besides sight and hearing to determine if you're dead are unaffected by this.

POWER STRIKE
[Might Below 7, Unarmed Combat Training Feat] (1pt)
Your character is very confident in their first strike. In combat you get +3 damage ignoring armor to your first unarmed melee attack.

PROTECTED MIND
[Vitality Below 7] (4pt)
Your character has some reason that their mind is more protected from SCP. This could be anything from mental training, to a metal plate being put into their head, or maybe because of the influence of another SCP in their past. Either way this character takes half strain from mind effects and only takes half sanity damage.

QUICK DRAW
[Agility Below 7] (1pt)
Your character has amazingly fast reaction time. As such when drawing or switching weapons you no longer have to take an action. Reloading now takes 1 action instead of a round.

Date: 25/10/████████

Document security clearance level: Class B

Level 0 ☐   Level 1 ☐   Level 2 ☒   Level 3 ☐   Level 4 ☐

SCP KNOWLEDGE
[Class C or B] (1-5pt)
Your character has studied or worked around specific SCP for a while. As such you know these SCP like the back of your hand, including all notes presented and researched on them. You recognize 1-5 SCP (1pt per SCP), which allows you to up to 5 times over the course of the game tell the GM "I know this SCP". In these situations he gives you all the information on the chosen SCP. This uses one of your SCP knowledges permanently. Only one player should have this feat.

SECURITY PASSES
[Class C or above] (1pt)
Your character has higher level security passes for some reason. be it that they have connections further up in the facility, or they got lucky and found one. Either way you get security clearance through areas 1 security level higher than your class; however if caught using a pass with security above your authorization level you will be demoted, and in some cases memory wiped and named a Class D.

SHIELDING
[Might Below 7] (1pt)
You are good at finding things to defend yourself with. When using a shield or an object like a shield, you get +1 to +10 Armor based on the object and the GM's decision. This armor only counts for things you can feasibly block with the object, and if the object takes more damage than it's armor it breaks. Taking cover with this skill also makes the enemy take a -2 on shots against you.

SIGN LANGUAGE
[None] (1pt)
Your character can communicate with others that have this feat without words, over any visual distance.

SNEAKY
[Agility Below 7] (3pt)
Sneaky characters can surprise others easy. They get the ability to Surprise others in combat. This gives a sneaky character initiative in all combat where they are not seen before the first round, plus a free pre-combat action.

SPRINTER
[Agility Below 8] (1pt)
When not carrying more than 10lbs (besides clothing), your character gains +5ft to movespeed and +10ft to sprinting speed.

STRESSLESS LIVING
[Experience Below 9, or Smarts Below 9] (3pt)
Your character is great at dealing with stress. As such stressful situations effect them less. When moving up the stress track they only move half (moving 1 point up the stress track does not effect you at all).

SURVIVAL TRAINING
[Vitality Below 9] (1pt)
You know how to live in unfavorable circumstance. As such you can take Survival checks to find food, water, or navigate in situations where these things would otherwise not be available to you.

THICK SKIN
[Vitality Below 8] (2pt)
Your character reduces damage done to them (after armor) by 1. Their skin is also resistant to cutting, bullets, and other forms of non-combat damage. Non combat damage under 3 does nothing to you.

TRIP
[None] (1pt)
You are a tricky bugger who fights dirty. Whether it be your friends or enemies you are willing to stick a foot out in front of them and take them down. Performing a Trip check (using Agility) successfully drops your target prone should they fail an Agility save to prevent it.

UNARMED COMBAT TRAINING
[Might Below 9] (1pt)
Your character is good at fighting bare handed or with simple brawling tools like brass knuckles. As such you get +1 to unarmed melee combat.

WEAPON MASTERY (BLADES)
[Might Below 6, Weapon Training (Blades)] (2pt)
Your character is good with melee weapons. You are familiar with all forms of blades such as swords, daggers, etc. As such you get +2 to use such a weapon.

WEAPON MASTERY (BOWS)
[Agility Below 7, Weapon Training (Bows)] (2pt)
Your character is good with ranged weapons. You are familiar with all forms of bows, crossbows, and ranged bow or blowgun weapons. As such you get +2 to use such a weapon.

WEAPON MASTERY (CLUBS/MACES/HAMMERS)
[Might Below 7, Weapon Training (Clubs/Maces/Hammers)] (2pt)
Your character is good with melee weapons. You are familiar with all forms of clubs, maces, hammers, etc. As such you get +2 to use such a weapon.

WEAPON MASTERY (EXPLOSIVES)
[Agility Below 8, Smarts Below 7, Weapon Training (Explosives) Feat] (2pt)
Your character is good with explosives such as dynamite, C4, Gernades, and RPG's. As such you get +2 on rolls to use such weapons.

WEAPON MASTERY (GUNS)
[Agility Below 6, Weapon Training (Guns) Feat] (2pt)
Your character is good with ranged weapons. You are familiar with all forms of guns, be it rifles, pistols, SMG's, etc. As such you get +2 to use such a weapon.

WEAPON MASTERY (SPECIAL)
[Smarts Below 6, Weapon Training (Special) Feat] (2pt)
Your character is good with special weapons. You are familiar with all forms of foundation gear, and scp weaponry. As such you get +2 to use such a weapon.

Secure. Contain. Protect.

Date: 25/10/███████

Document security clearance level: Class B

Level 0 ☐   Level 1 ☐   Level 2 ☑   Level 3 ☐   Level 4 ☐

WEAPON TRAINING (BLADES)
[Might Below 8] (1pt)
Your character is good with melee weapons.
You are familiar with all forms of blades such
as swords, daggers, etc. As such you get no
negatives to use such a weapon.

WEAPON TRAINING (BOWS)
[Agility Below 9] (1pt)
Your character is good with ranged weapons.
You are familiar with all forms of bows,
crossbows, and ranged bow or blowgun
weapons. As such you get no negatives to use
such a weapon.

WEAPON TRAINING (CLUBS/MACES/HAMMERS)
[Might Below 9] (1pt)
Your character is good with melee weapons.
You are familiar with all forms of clubs, maces,
hammers, etc. As such you get no negatives to
use such a weapon.

WEAPON TRAINING (EXPLOSIVES)
[Agility Below 9, Smarts Below 9] (2pt)
Your character is good with explosives such as
dynamite, C4, Gernades, and RPG's. As such
you get no negatives to use such weapons.

WEAPON TRAINING (GUNS)
[Agility Below 8] (2pt)
Your character is good with ranged weapons.
You are familiar with all forms of guns, be it
rifles, pistols, SMG's, etc. As such you get no
negatives to use such a weapon.

WEAPON TRAINING (SPECIAL)
[Smarts Below 8, Class C or above] (2pt)
Your character is good with special weapons.
You are familiar with all forms of foundation
and SCP weapons. As such you get no
negatives to use such a weapon.

SCP

Secure. Contain. Protect.

Date: 25/10/ ██████

Document security clearance level: Class B

Level 0 ☐   Level 1 ☐   Level 2 ☒   Level 3 ☐   Level 4 ☐

FLAWS

ADDICTION (CAFFEINE)
[Vitality Above 9] (1pt)
Your character needs caffeine at least once a day. Drinking caffeine will give your character +1 to smarts rolls for 1 hour and sate them for the day. Failing to drink caffeine in 24 hours will give the character a -1 to all smarts rolls until they drink some caffeine.

ADDICTION (ALCOHOL)
[Vitality Above 9] (2pt)
Your character needs alcohol at least once a day. Having any form of alcohol will sate them for the day, but also give them -1 to experience rolls for the next hour. Failing to have any alcohol in 24 hours will give the character a -1 to all agility and might rolls until they have alcohol.

ADDICTION (CIGARETTES)
[Vitality Above 9] (3pt)
Your character needs cigarettes at least once a day. Having any form of cigarette will sate them for the day. Failing to have any cigarettes in 24 hours will give the character a -2 to all agility and might rolls until they have a cigarette.

ADDICTION (MARIJUANA)
[Vitality Above 9] (4pt)
Your character needs marijuana at least once a day. Having any form of it will sate them for the day, giving them -2 to experience and smarts rolls for the next hour. Failing to have any in 24 hours will give the character a -3 to all agility and might rolls until they have some.

ADDICTION (HEROIN)
[Vitality Above 9] (5pt)
Your character needs heroin at least once a day. Having any form of it will sate them for the day, and give them -4 to experience and smarts rolls for the next 2 hours. Failing to have any in 24 hours will give the character a -6 to all agility and might rolls until they have some heroin.

ALLERGIES
[Vitality Above 13] (2pt)
You are afflicted with allergies. These may be something as simple as hay fever, but the reactions to such will result in something like a huge bout of sneezing and gasping, and will cause a temporary -2 to both Might and Vitality rolls during the fit, as well as making you unable to dodge for the duration. This can be activated by the GM once per game for the duration of an encounter.

ALOOF
[Smarts Below 7] (2pt)
Your manner is cold and unapproachable, distancing you from friends and strangers alike. Your preternatural intelligence lends itself to viewing others as slow-witted and a waste of your precious time. This gives a -2 to all influence rolls on everyone above your smarts skill.

Date: 25/10/██████

Document security clearance level: Class B

Level 0 ☐   Level 1 ☐   Level 2 ☒   Level 3 ☐   Level 4 ☐

AMNESIA
[Experience Above 14] (2-6pt)
You are unable to remember anything about your past, yourself, or your family. Your life is a blank slate. However, your past may someday come back to haunt you. You must take 1-3 other flaws without choosing what they are. The GM will supply the details over the course of the campaign. You and your character will slowly discover them. 1 Flaw = 2pt, 2 Flaws = 4pt, 3 Flaws = 6pt.

BAD HEALTH
[Vitality Above 14] (2pt)
You are always in bad health, and tend to get diseases easier and recover slower. As such when resting or bandaging wounds, you take twice as long to heal any ailment.

BAD KARMA
[Influence Above 11, or Experience above 11] (2pt)
A character with this flaw has lived a bad life of kicking puppies, feeding people spoiled food, and probably stealing and killing. they are hunted by bad luck and karma and as such only move half up the karma track (moving 1 up the karma track does nothing), but move double up the curse track.

BAD REPUTATION
[Influence Above 13] (2pt)
You have a reputation that angers or frightens people. Examples include being unlucky, petty, or cruel. The rep may or may not be accurate, but in either case, word travels faster than you do. You suffer a -2 penalty to all Influence rolls against other humans. In addition, when checks are made to influence NPC attitudes, you can never attain a rating higher than Friendly, no matter how well you roll or how long you've known someone.

BLIND
[None] (4pt)
You are completely blind, and fail all rolls that involve vision. You also suffer the normal gaming penalties for blindness. You were born without the capacity to see (whether or not you actually have eyes is up to you), and therefore can never be healed. With the GM's approval, a SCP, Experiment, or Miracle may correct this flaw.

BLOOD ON YOUR HANDS
[Might Below 9] (1pt)
Your character is stronger than they look, and forget this fact a lot. When trying to do something delicate, or trying to perform non lethal actions in combat, the GM rolls 1D4. on a 1-2 you accidentally use too much force and deal lethal damage, or perform a loud powerful action instead of being delicate with what you were working on.

Date: 25/10/█████████

Document security clearance level: Class B

Level 0 ☐   Level 1 ☐   Level 2 ☑   Level 3 ☐   Level 4 ☐

BRANDED
[Must be Taken as Class D] (1pt)
You have been marked a Class D and now have a prominent brand. You may have been a criminal, a slave, or some other such illicit individual before being brought to the foundation. The brand is such that it cannot be easily covered, and a search reveals it each time. Law enforcement agents of any higher level personnel immediately take you into custody or execute you if they see the mark on you outside of containment. It is your choice as to whether or not you were falsely accused of the crime that initially put you on death row.

BREEDS ENVY
[Influence Below 8] (2pt)
Your phenomenal Charisma or Appearance breeds jealousy and envy wherever you go, spurring resentment in many people. This causes sudden changes in attitude when trying to convince people to work with you or be friendly. This flaw changes your critical failure range on Influence rolls to 1-3. If a 1-3 is rolled during these tests the target of the test will become hostile instead of friendly.

BREEDS POSSESSIVENESS
[Influence Below 8] (1pt)
Your Charisma or Appearance makes you the object of people's desire wherever you travel, tempting others to win your devotion at any cost--even if they have to lock you in a tower or kill your companions in order to persuade you. This flaw changes your critical failure range on influence rolls to 1-3.

If a 1-3 is rolled when interacting with an NPC they will become obsessed with you, and desire to make you theirs by taking away everything else you have.

BROKEN LIMB
[None] (2pt+1pt per Additional Limb)
Your limb is damaged and causes you pain when using it. If it is an arm you take -3 to checks while using that arm, and move two up the strain track. If it is a leg you must move at 1/2 speed and cannot sprint. If you try to run or walk at full speed you gain 2 strain.

BRUISE EASILY
[Might Above 12] (1pt)
Each time you take bludgeoning damage, including that from falls, you take an extra point of damage per damage die against you.

BUSYBODY
[Experience Below 8] (1pt)
What is the point of having so much intelligence and stored knowledge if you can't show people the error of their ways? You share your experience with others even when it's not wanted or needed. As such when a party member or NPC working with the party fails a difficult task (Determined by the GM) you start monologuing to them about the correct way to perform the task. This makes the difficulty of their task increase by adding -3 to their roll because of the distraction.

Date: 25/10/▮▮▮▮▮

Document security clearance level: Class B

Level 0 ☐   Level 1 ☐   Level 2 ☒   Level 3 ☐   Level 4 ☐

CARELESS
[None] (2pt)
For some reason, people always seem to escape your clutches. You don't understand how that's possible. After all, you throw them into your easily escapable deathtraps before leaving them alone with your bumbling guards while you wander away for no apparent reason. Once per game session, the GM or another player can activate this Flaw in order for an NPC or another player to succeed automatically at a skill or ability check during an escape from you, one of your traps, or one of your prisons. In addition, you suffer a -2 penalty to any checks involving the creation of items or the like, including such things as binding someone with rope or chain. You just can't manage to do a great job at anything.

CAUTIOUS
[None] (1pt)
You are uneasy engaging in behavior that carries a chance of failure. You must spend twice as long performing any skill that requires an action. For example, deciphering a page of text would take 2 minutes for you instead of 1. In addition, you suffer a -2 penalty on Initiative rolls.

CLASS E SECRET
[Cannot be Class A] (4pt)
The character is secretly a Class E subject (sometimes even to themselves) and have already been affected by an SCP in a severe way. The GM may activate this flaw at a later time to cause a SCP's effect on this character once per game without resistance saves.

CLUMSINESS
[Agility Above 12] (2pt)
You have the unfortunate habit of dropping things, knocking things over, or tripping. Once per game session, the GM or another player can activate this flaw in order to cause your clumsiness to come into effect at a crucial moment, which results in a failed check, attack, or the like. In addition, you suffer a -1 penalty to all Might and Agility based skill or ability checks at all times.

COLOURBLIND
[None] (1pt)
Though this is a misconception, for game purposes, you see everything in black, white, and shades of gray.

COMPULSIVE HONESTY
[None] (2pt)
You cannot tell a lie, nor can you behave in a deceitful fashion. You tend to be blunt rather than tactful, even if it means insulting someone who you and your companions are trying to impress. If it is a matter of life and death, you may make an influence save at -3 to your roll to speak or act out a falsehood. However, if successful, you suffer a -4 penalty to all attack rolls, saves, and skill checks for the next 1D4 hours due to feelings of guilt.

Date: 25/10/▮▮▮▮

Document security clearance level: Class B

Level 0 ☐ Level 1 ☐ Level 2 ☒ Level 3 ☐ Level 4 ☐

COWARDLY
[Cautious Flaw] (2pt)
You have a strong sense of self-preservation. You often hesitate to put yourself at risk, even if there's a good reason to do so. In dangerous circumstances, you are likely to run away. You automatically fail all saves against Fear effects of any sort. An ability that makes you immune to fear instead grants you a saving throw, but at a -4 penalty on the save.

CURIOSITY
[Smarts Below 10] (2pt)
You're a naturally curious person and you find mysteries of any sort irresistible. In most circumstances, alas, your curiosity overrides your common sense. Once per game session, the DM or another player can activate this flaw to force you to investigate something unusual, even if it looks like it might be dangerous. In addition, you suffer a -2 penalty to checks such as apposed Influence checks when being seduced, being tricked into a trap of some sort, or any similar situation in which your curiosity can be piqued and may outweigh your better judgment.

CURSED FAMILY (MAJOR)
[None] (2pt)
Your character has always felt cursed, and as such starts with 2 points in the curse track. these points can be used by the GM as normal once per session, but they do not go away on use.

CURSED FAMILY (MINOR)
[None] (1pt)
Your character has always felt cursed, and as such starts with 1 point in the curse track. this point can be used by the GM as normal once per session, but it does not go away on use.

DEAFNESS
[None] (3pt)
You cannot hear sound--you can feel the vibrations of very loud noises, nothing more. As you were born without the capacity to hear, this condition cannot be healed by most means...at least by nothing short of a Miracle or SCP Experiment. In game terms, you suffer the penalties for the Deafened condition at all times. On the upside, there are some specific attack forms which you would suffer no or reduced damage and effects from.

DEEP SLEEPER
[None] (1pt)
You are only awakened by extremely loud noises, or being physically shaken, prodded, etc. Even when you do wake up, you spend 1D4 rounds able to do nothing other than try to shake the cobwebs away and groggily sit up. During this time, if you need to defend yourself, you are considered unable to dodge or use agility saves, despite any feats or profession features you may have that would indicate otherwise.

Date: 25/10/██████

Document security clearance level: Class B

Level 0 ☐   Level 1 ☐   Level 2 ☒   Level 3 ☐   Level 4 ☐

EXHAUSTED EASILY
[Might above 11, or Vitality above 11] (2pt)
A character with this flaw has no endurance whatsoever. They might be strong, agile, or generally healthy in other ways, but it is always in short bursts. As such these characters strain themselves easier and move double up the strain track.

FANATIC
[None] (2pt)
Your character has become obsessed with a religion, belief, or 'deity' that they believe is their 'god'. This could be a particular set of beliefs, a specific SCP or person, or any number of things. This feat requires great role play to pull off, and the player will perform immoral or unorthodox actions for their beliefs, or listen to their 'god' unwaveringly. You get a -5 to all checks to resist your urge to follow your beliefs even at the cost of safety and your friends.

FRAGILE SKELETON
[Might above 11, Vitality above 11] (2pt)
Due to some deficiency with vitamins, exercise, or genetics; your skeleton is fragile and lacking density. As such bludgeoning damage done to you does double, and lower your Health on each body part by 1.

GENERALIZED ANXIETY DISORDER (MOTOR TENSION)
[None] (4pt)
Jitteriness, aches, twitches, restlessness, easily startled, easily fatigued, and so on. All dodge saves, and all checks involving Might, Agility, and Vitality take a -3 penalty.

GENERALIZED ANXIETY DISORDER (AUTONOMIC HYPERACTIVITY)
[None] (1pt)
Sweating, racing heart, dizziness, clammy hands, flushed or pallid face, rapid pulse and respiration even when at rest, and so on. All saves, and skill checks take a -1 penalty.

GENERALIZED ANXIETY DISORDER (EXPECTATIONS OF DOOM)
[None] (2pt)
Anxieties, worries, fears, and especially anticipations of misfortune. All attack rolls, and skill checks take a -2 penalty.

GENERALIZED ANXIETY DISORDER (VIGILANCE)
[None] (3pt)
Distraction, inability to focus, insomnia, irritability, impatience. All Experience saves and checks involving Smarts, Experience, or Influence suffer a -3 penalty.

GLORY SEEKER
[Experience Above 13] (2pt)
Your character is a glutton for glory. they want all the recognition of being the hero, and as such jump into combat situations where success is sometimes not even an option. As such you cannot disengage from combat unless you take 2 stress and pass a experience check, or you beat the opponent into submission.

Date: 25/10/███████

Document security clearance level: Class B

Level 0 ☐   Level 1 ☐   Level 2 ☒   Level 3 ☐   Level 4 ☐

GREEDY
[None] (1pt)
Your character likes money and loot a lot. They are willing to risk a lot to get the most. When money or goods are on the line your character will go for them. When being offered a 'shared pay' with a team of players, you will fight to get the loot all for yourself. you can take an experience check and 2 stress to avoid attacking friends for their loot once per 'loot grabbing' opportunity.

INATTENTIVE
[Smarts Above 11] (2pt)
Your character lacks an attention span needed to perform a lot of tasks. As such when performing a task the GM may roll 1D4. On a 2 you lose focus on your task and it takes 2x as long to perform, on a 1 you forget what your were doing and have to start the task over after half the normal tasks duration.

INDECISIVE
[None] (2pt)
Your character cannot make split second or important decisions without stressing over them for a period of time. If the player with this flaw is forced to make an important decision quickly, they cannot and lose all initiative for that round or combat forcing them to go last, hopefully having their decision made for them by the rest of the group. If they still do not know what to do (ex. no direction from teammates, friends, or even the enemies), then they take 2 stress to return to normal and make the decision themselves.

INJURED LIMB
[None] (1pt, +0.5pt per Additional Limb)
Your limb is damaged and causes you pain when using it. If it is an arm you take -1 to checks while using that arm, and move one up the strain track. If it is a leg you must move at 3/4 speed and cannot sprint. If you try to run or walk at full speed you gain 1 strain.

INSOMNIAC
[Vitality Above 10] (1pt)
Your character has a hard time getting a full nights rest. As such they cannot recover fully from a rest as they will never get an unbroken 8 hours normally. When trying to sleep the Insomniac rolls 2D4 and then sleep for that many hours. If they roll an 7-8, then they recover all stats normally. If they roll less they must move up the stress, strain, or curse scales (in any amount divided between them), equal to half the number of hours they lost trying to sleep. they also only recover up to 3/4 their maximum Health and Sanity. An example would be rolling 4 hours, so by losing 4 hours of sleep you must move 2 points up your tracks. I move one up in strain, and one up in stress.

INTOLERANCE
[None] (1pt)
You really dislike some class of person, animal, or situation that you judge is wrong. This causes you to take a -4 penalty to rolls involving your intolerance, such as talking with a person from that class you don't like, or attempting to avoid the animal you cant stand.

Date: 25/10/██████

Document security clearance level: Class B

Level 0 ☐   Level 1 ☐   Level 2 ☒   Level 3 ☐   Level 4 ☐

JUMPS TO CONCLUSIONS
[Experience Above 12] (1pt)
Your character has a great eye for detail, but because of this doesn't believe they can do things if there is no answer they can see. When checking for a solution to a door, puzzle, or searching a room; if your character fails their check, they conclude that the thing they searched for doesn't exist, or that the puzzle is impossible to solve, and will not attempt it again.

LAZY
[Vitality Above 12] (2pt)
Your character will not do anything that isn't absolutely necessary. they will avoid even important tasks for survival just to get a few extra minutes of sleep. As such in order to stop laying around and perform skills outside of life threatening situations, you take 1 strain. This 1 strain is gained every time you do a new task.

LECHEROUS
[None] (1pt)
You have a lusty nature and a tendency to pursue the pleasures of the flesh. A pretty woman or a handsome man (however your tastes run) is an almost irresistible temptation to you. Once per game session, the GM or another player can activate your Flaw in order to convince you to give in to temptation. In addition you get -2 to any saves to try and avoid being seduced.

MISSING LIMB
[None] (4pt, +2pt per Additional Limb)
Your limb is gone entirely and canot be used. If it was an arm that went missing, then you cannot perform checks that require that arm or both arms. If it is a leg that has gone missing you must move at 1/2 speed and cannot sprint, or even attempt to move faster.

MOOD DISORDER (DEPRESSION)
[None] (2pt)
Symptoms of this illness include changes in appetite, weight gain or loss, too much or too little sleep, persistent feeling of tiredness or sluggishness, and feelings of worthlessness or guilt, leading in severe cases to hallucinations, delusions, stupor, or thoughts of suicide. All attack rolls, saves, and checks take a -2 penalty. A predisposition to use alcohol or other mood-altering substances in an attempt at self-medication exists. You can gain a stress point to avoid the -2 penalty for the next 10min.

MOOD DISORDER (MANIA)
[None] (2pt)
The character has a fairly constant euphoric or possibly irritable mood. Symptoms include a general increase in activity, talkativeness, increased self-esteem to the point of delusion, decreased need for sleep, being easily distracted, willingness for dangerous or imprudent activities , delusions, hallucinations, and bizarre behavior. All attack rolls, saves, and checks take a -2 penalty. A predisposition to use alcohol or other substances in an attempt at self-medication exists. You can gain a stress point to avoid the -2 penalty for the next 10min.

MOOD DISORDER (BIPOLAR)
[None] (4pt)
The character oscillates between the mood states mentioned above, sometimes staying in one mood for weeks at a time, sometimes rapidly switching from one to another. Also known as manic depressive. You take a -3 at all times instead of -2, and it takes 2 stress to remove the negative for 5min.

MORAL CODE (CHIVALROUS COURTESY)
[Influence Below 10] (2pt)
You despise raising your hand against creatures of the opposite gender. You suffer a -3 penalty on attack rolls to hit a creature that you can tell is of the opposite gender.

MORAL CODE (CODE OF ARMS)
[Influence Below 10] (2pt)
Trained to only kill other armed fighters, you hesitate when attacking unarmed opponents. You suffer a -3 penalty on attack rolls made against an enemy not armed with a weapon. If the enemy uses a natural or unarmed attack against you, you may then attack it without penalty.

MORAL CODE (THE DUEL)
[Influence Below 10] (2pt)
You only cross arms with foes who willingly engage you. You suffer a -3 attack penalty on attack rolls against creatures that have not explicitly challenged you or made an attack against you. For the purposes of this flaw, an attack against you includes any action that would end an Invisibility of any kind.

MORAL CODE (FACE ME)
[Influence Below 10] (2pt)
You prefer to fight someone face to face. You gain no benefit from flanking a foe and instead suffer a -3 penalty on rolls made against a foe you flank.

MUTE
[None] (2pt)
You cannot speak or voice any sound. You can only communicate through written word or by using sign language if you have the sign language feat.

NIGHT BLINDNESS
[Agility Above 11] (1pt)
Your character is blind in the dark. They only have 1/4 their visual range in low light, and are considered blind in pitch darkness.

NIGHTMARES
[None] (1pt)
Your character has constant vivid nightmares when they sleep. Whenever this character sleeps the GM rolls 1D4, on a 1 they have a nightmare that makes them yell in their sleep, and after waking they will have -1 to all rolls for the remainder of the day.

OBESE
[Might Above 12, Agility Above 14, Out of Shape Flaw] (2pt)
Your character is physically incapable of most work do to their stature. They get -3 to rolls requiring physical work (Replacing the Out of Shape -1).

SCP

Date: 25/10/▮▮▮▮▮

Document security clearance level: Class B

Level 0 ☐   Level 1 ☐   Level 2 ☒   Level 3 ☐   Level 4 ☐

OCD: OBSESSIONS
[None] (3pt)
The character cannot help thinking about an idea, image, or impulse incessantly, often involving violence and self-doubt. These ideas are frequently repugnant to the character, but they are so strong that during times of stress (such as combat) she may be unable to concentrate on anything else, even if doing so is necessary for her survival. As such they take -2 to all checks that involve concentration due to being preoccupied by thoughts of your obsession, you may gain 1 stress to avoid those thoughts for 10min and not have the negative apply.

OCD: COMPULSIONS
[None] (5pt)
The character insists on performing ritual actions, such as touching a doorway at left, right, and top before passing through it. Though she may agree that the actions are senseless, the need to perform them is overpowering and may last for up to 10 rounds (1d10, rolled for each specific instance). Your character can avoid this compulsion for 10min by gaining 2 stress, and avoid the negatives that apply. While performing your compulsion you cannot stop or take other actions, without taking the 2 stress to force yourself to stop prematurely.

ONE-EYED
[None] (1pt)
Your character is missing an eye. you have no peripheral vision on one side (your choice), and get -2 when performing ranged attacks from guns to throwing, or anything of similar challenge to your depth perception.

OUT OF SHAPE
[Agility Above 12] (1pt)
A character with the out of shape flaw is physically below the average person. Out of shape characters get -1 to rolls requiring physical work.

OVERCONFIDENT
[Influence Above 10] (2pt)
Nothing is beyond your capabilities. If you wanted, you could defeat the best swordsman in the world; you just haven't had any reason to do so yet. And surely that chasm isn't too wide for you to leap across. Once per game session, the GM or another player can activate your Flaw once a session in order to squash any doubts you may have had about your own capabilities.

PACIFIST
[None] (1pt)
You are a pacifist and will not kill anyone. All of your attacks must be in self defense, and even then they must be non lethal.

Date: 25/10/████████

Document security clearance level: Class B

Level 0 ☐   Level 1 ☐   Level 2 ☑   Level 3 ☐   Level 4 ☐

PARTIER
[Vitality Below 10] (1pt)
Your character loves to have a good time. They party way too much, eat too much, and drink too much. They have an impossible time trying to resist the invitation to party anytime anywhere. Once per game the GM can call upon this flaw to make you drop your guard and join a party. You also get -3 to influence rolls to seduce or charm you into partying.

PERSONALITY DISORDER
[None] (2pt)
All personality disorders will cause a -3 to all influence checks due to your character being hard to interact with normally. The choices on personalities are below:
ANTISOCIAL: Short-sighted and reckless behavior, habitual liar, confrontational, fails to meet obligations (job, bills, relationships), disregards rights and feelings of others.
AVOIDANCE: Oversensitive to rejection, low self-esteem, socially withdrawn.
BORDERLINE: Rapid mood shifts, impulsive, unable to control temper, chronic boredom.
COMPULSIVE: Perfectionist, authoritarian, indecisive from fear of making mistakes, difficulty expressing emotions.
DEPENDENT: Lacks self-confidence, seeks another to look up to, follow, and subordinate herself to ("codependent").
HISTRIONIC: Overly dramatic, craves attention and excitement, overreacts, displays temper tantrums, may threaten suicide if thwarted.
NARCISSISTIC: Exaggerated sense of self-importance, craves attention and admiration, considers others' rights and feelings as of lesser importance.

PASSIVE-AGGRESSIVE: Procrastinator, stubborn, intentionally forgetful, deliberately inefficient, sabotages own performance on a regular basis. PARANOID: Jealous, easily offended, suspicious, humorless, secretive, vigilant, exaggerates magnitude of offenses against oneself, refuses to accept blame. SCHIZOID: Emotionally cold, aloof, has few friends, indifferent to praise or criticism.

PHOBIA
[None] (2pt)
A character afflicted by a phobia persistently fears a particular object or situation. She realizes that the fear is excessive and irrational, but the fear is disturbing enough that she avoids the stimulus. As such running into something that correlated to your phobia will cause you to move up the fear track twice as fast.

PRIDEFUL
[Influence Above 12] (1pt)
Your character is too proud in themselves to accept help. They will take 1 stress to receive help from others in most circumstances, but if they receive a pity assistance of any kind they will outright refuse it.

RAVENOUS APPETITE
[Might below 8, or Vitality below 8] (3pt)
You need to eat a lot to keep up your muscle mass and health. As such you requires 3x the normal food and water intake as a normal person. Not recieving the proper amount of food in a day will cause you to get -2 to all rolls and +1 strain stacking for each additional day without the proper amount of food.

Date: 25/10/███████

Document security clearance level: Class B

Level 0 ☐   Level 1 ☐   Level 2 ☒   Level 3 ☐   Level 4 ☐

SCP TARGET
[None] (2pt)
Your character inexplicably attracts SCP to them. This is both good when trying to find harmless or helpful SCP, but terrible when Keter and other dangerous SCP hunt you. The GM will make SCP target you more often, and be able to roll to track you based on luck alone.

SHAKEN
[None] (2pt)
You had experienced something that had shaken you in the past and it haunts you until this day. As such you start with 1 point in the Fear track, but this point in fear can never be removed.

SHORT WINDED
[Vitality Above 12] (1pt)
You do not have a lot of stamina and get winded easily. You can only run for 2 rounds maximum, and get exhausted after 3 rounds of combat. If you get exhausted in either case you must rest for 5min or take -1 to all rolls for each additional run or round of combat until you rest.

SHY
[Influence Above 13] (2pt)
You are distinctly ill at ease when dealing with people, and you try to avoid social situations whenever possible. All rolls concerned with social dealings are made with a -3 penalty, and any roll your character makes while being the center of attention is made at a -6 penalty. Don't expect to make any public speeches.

SQUEAMISH
[Vitality Above 12] (1pt)
Your character is easily upset by gross, bloody, or terrifying situations. As such any situation involving the aforementioned causes your character to move 1 up the fear and strain track because of the mental and physical strain you experience.

STRESSED LIVING
[Experience above 11, or Smarts above 11] (2pt)
A character like this is always stressed out over every little thing. They stress out over others, themselves, and sometimes even nothing. As such they move double up the stress track.

TALKATIVE
[Influence Above 11] (1pt)
You have a problem keeping your plans to yourself. Your ideas are simply so clever that you tell them to other people, so that you can watch their astonishment creep across their faces just before they tell you just how smart you are. The GM can activate your flaw in order to get you to reveal your plan to the wrong people. When a plan comes together you have to pass a influence test at -2 to avoid blurting your plan out to others nearby.

Date: 25/10/██████████

Document security clearance level: Class B

Level 0 ☐   Level 1 ☐   Level 2 ☒   Level 3 ☐   Level 4 ☐

TONGUE TIED
[Influence Above 13] (2pt)
This disadvantage comes up whenever you try to discuss anything of importance and relay pressing information and such. You have the tendency to incorrectly state facts, forget or mix up names, and generally say the wrong thing. At GM's discretion, you can suffer a -3 penalty on social interactions to relay important information.

TRUSTING
[Influence Above 12] (2pt)
You don't like to believe that other people are capable of misleading and lying to you. After all, people are basically good, right?. Once per game session, the GM or another player can activate your Flaw in order to quell any doubts you may have about another person. In addition, anyone attempting to persuade you via the Influence skill gains a +3 bonus to the attempt.

UN-REACTIVE
[Agility Above 14] (1pt)
You are particularly slow at reacting to danger and other stimuli. As such, you suffer a -5 penalty on all Initiative checks.

VULNERABLE
[Vitality Above 13] (2pt)
You are not very good at defending yourself and moving out of harm's way. In game terms, you suffer a constant -1 to all armor locations and to all Dodge saves.

Date: 25/10/ ████████

Document security clearance level: Class D

Level 0 ☒   Level 1 ☐   Level 2 ☐   Level 3 ☐   Level 4 ☐

CHAPTER 6 - EQUIPMENT

In this chapter we will be outlining the equipment available within the Foundation. This equipment may or may not be available to you based on your Classification within the Foundation. Please skip any Equipment not for your level. Specialty Equipment is off limits to all non Military Personal as some of it could **[REDACTED]**.

Equipment is sectioned by type, relative damage potential, and restrictions. We have also listed common locations within our facility to help you find this equipment should you be authorized to use it, and require it for testing or otherwise.

TABLE 6-1: GENERAL EQUIPMENT

EQUIPMENT	Weight	Additional Functionality	Restrictions
Clip Boards	N/A	Can keep notes together on a single clip board.	None
Office Supplies	N/A	General office supplies for pens, markers, tape, etc.	None
Backpack (Standard)	2lbs	Increases Carry weight of personnel by 50lbs	None
Backpack (Military)	4lbs	Increases carry weight of personnel by 150lbs.	Class C and Above
Storage Crate	10lbs + Contents	Can hold up to 3ft x 3ft of contents weighing over 500 lbs.	None
Rope	1lb / 5ft	A length of rope used to tie, to route things.	Class C and Above
Chain	3lbs / 5ft	A length of chain used to attach heavy equipment, or tie things down.	Class C and Above
Flashlight	1lb	Lights up an area equal to around 20ft in front of the user, in a cone shape.	Class C or Above
Security Pass	N/A	Used to access security doors of your Security Level.	Class C or Above
Batteries	N/A	1 set of batteries that last 4 hours of continuous use, for flashlights or other electronic gear.	None

SCP

Secure. Contain. Protect.

Date: 25/10/▮▮▮▮▮

Document security clearance level: Class C

Level 0 ☐   Level 1 ☒   Level 2 ☐   Level 3 ☐   Level 4 ☐

TABLE 6-2: ARMOR & CLOTHING

Certain Armor can be requisitioned for Class D, but under normal circumstance only Class C or above will have access to this table.

ARMOR	Weight	AV	Location	Additional Functionality	Restrictions
Medical Gloves	0.5 lbs	N/A	Arms	Gives protection from diseases / contact containments.	None
Medical Mask	0.1 lbs	N/A	Head	Gives protection from liquid / contact containments. 10% chance to resist airborne.	None
Gas Mask	2lbs	4	Head	Gives immunity to liquid, contact, and airborne containments that can be filtered.	Military / Requisition
Oxygen Mask	3lbs	3	Head	Gives immunity to all containments for 1 hour per O2 container.	Requisition
Hazard Suit	5lbs	3/Loc.	All	Immune to airborne, liquid, and contact containments. This effect is removed if any part of the armor is breached.	Requisition
Metal Mesh Gloves	5lbs	5/Arm	Arms	Immune to blades to arms. Take 1 damage from small firearms or arrows to the arms. -1 Agility Rolls	Military
Metal Mesh Legs	7lbs	5/Leg	Legs	Immune to blades to legs. Take 1 damage from small firearms, bows, or bludgeoning weapons. -1 Agility Rolls	Military
Metal Mesh Vest	10lbs	10	Body	Immune to blades to Body. Take 1 damage from small firearms, bows, or bludgeoning weapons. -1 Agility Rolls	Military
Military Helmet	2lbs	5	Head	Immune to blades to head. Take 1 damage from small firearms, bows, or bludgeoning weapons.	Military
Arm Ammo Holster	1lbs	1/Arm	Arms	Carry 2 extra clips of ammo per arm for small firearms, or 1 extra clip per arm for larger guns.	Military
Kevlar Vest	3lbs	12	Body	Take 1 damage from all medium or lower firearms, and non blade melee weapons.	Military
Fiber Mesh Pants	2lbs	4/leg	Legs	Take 1 damage from all medium or lower firearms, and non blade melee weapons.	Military
Night-vision Gear	1lb	N/A	Accessory	Attaches to head armor to allow night vision to see straight ahead with full vision in absolute darkness.	Military

Date: 25/10/██████

Document security clearance level: Class C

Level 0 ☐   Level 1 ☒   Level 2 ☐   Level 3 ☐   Level 4 ☐

TABLE 6-3: MELEE WEAPONS

Melee weapons are to be used by security and military personnel only. Some can be requisitioned by class C personnel for testing purposes only, by O5 clearance.

Weapon	Weight	DMG	Type	Additional Functionality	Restrictions
Dagger	1 lb	1D4	Blade	N/A	Requisition
Machette	4 lbs	1D8	Blade	N/A	Military
Crovel Shovel	5 lbs	2D4	Blade, Club	Can dig large areas, and saw through things. Choose to use as a club or blade when using.	Requisition
Security Baton	2 lbs	1D4	Club	N/A	Military
Tazer Rod	3 lbs	1D4 Stun	Club	50% chance to stun on hit.	Military
Club	5 lbs	1D4	Club	N/A	Requisition

Date: 25/10/▮▮▮▮▮▮▮

Document security clearance level: Class C

Level 0 ☐   Level 1 ☐   Level 2 ☑   Level 3 ☐   Level 4 ☐

TABLE 6-4: RANGED WEAPONS

Ranged weapons are to be used by military personnel only. Certain Class C personnel can apply for permission to carry under O5 clearance.

Weapon	Weight	DMG	Type	Additional Functionality	Restrictions
Tazer	2 lbs	2 Stun	Small	Stuns at 75% chance. Range 20ft	Requisition, Military
Pistol	4 lbs	1D4	Small	Range 50ft	Military
Revolver	5 lbs	1D6	Small	Range 75ft	Military
SMG	7 lbs	2D4	Small	Range 50ft	Military
Rifle	10 lbs	2D6	Medium	Range 100ft	Military
Sniper	15 lbs	2D8	Heavy	Range 250ft	Military
Shotgun	10 lbs	1D8	Medium	Range 20ft x3 Dmg, 30ft x2 Dmg, 40ft x1 Dmg	Military
Grenade	2 lbs	3D6	Explosive	Range 20ft, 15ft x 15ft Explosion. Agility save 1/2 damage.	Military
Stun Grenade	3 lbs	1D4 Stun	Explosive	Range 20ft, 15ft x 15ft Stun Deafen Blind 1D4 rounds. Agility save to avoid.	Military
Smoke Grenade	3 lbs	N/A	Explosive	Range 20ft, 20ft x 20ft Smoke 2D4 rounds. 5ft vision in smoke, cannot see into smoke.	Military
Grenade Launcher	17 lbs	3D6	Heavy, Explosive	Range 50ft, 15ft x 15ft Explosion, Agility save 1/2 damage.	Military
RPG	20 lbs	3D8	Heavy, Explosive	Range 150ft, 15ft x 15ft Explosion, Agility save 1/2 damage.	Military

Date: 25/10/ ▓▓▓▓

Document security clearance level: Class B

Level 0 ☐   Level 1 ☐   Level 2 ☐   Level 3 ☒   Level 4 ☐

TABLE 6-5: SPECIAL WEAPONS

Special Weapons can only be used under breakout, containment, or O5 cleared special circumstances; and even then only by authorized military personnel.

Weapon	Weight	DMG	Type	Additional Functionality	Restrictions
Tazer Net	4 lbs	1D4 Stun	Utility	Stuns everything in 10ft x 10ft area in front of user at 75% chance.	Military
Energy Blade	5 lbs	2D6	Melee, Blade	Ignores AV 5 and below.	Special
Plasma Blade	3 lbs	2D8	Melee, Blade	Counts as Plasma Damage, Ignores AV 10 and below.	Special
Riot Shield	4 lbs	N/A	Utility, Shield	Adds 5 AV to your front. Hit with over 10 damage at once it breaks.	Military
Collapsing Shield	8 lbs	N/A	Utility, Shield	Adds 7 AV to your front and sides. Hit with over 14 damage at once it breaks. 1 turn to open and collapse.	Military
Plasma Shield	2 lbs	N/A	Utility, Shield	Ignore all damage from range. Uses 30min of battery charge per absorbed attack.	Special
Plasma Grenade	2 lbs	N/A	Explosive	Disintegrates matter inside the radius, resulting in death. 10ft x 10ft. Agility to avoid getting hit.	Special
ESP Enhancer	2 lbs	1D4	Utility	Allows the wielder to use a Mind attack to damage Sanity. Once equipped cannot be removed.	Special
ESP Shield	2 lbs	N/A	Utility	Gives the user a Smarts save against all Sanity Damage. Once equipped cannot be removed.	Special

CHAPTER 7 - COMBAT, MOVEMENT, SANITY, AND SPECIAL EFFECTS

In this Chapter will deal with the intricacies of life in the foundation. How you should move about, what you should do when found in an unfavorable situation, and how to deal with the effects of stress, mental breakdowns, and SCP related incidents. Information in this chapter will be broken down into "rounds" as a term of 6 second intervals.

COMBAT & MOVEMENT

Let us start off with the basics of combat and movement. When in the Facility movement is somewhat limited through our hallways and tight chamber rooms. This should not hinder you as much as you would think, but does make entering and leaving areas of the facility difficult without proper clearance. If you are a Class D member of the Foundation then you will only move about the facility as instructed.

We have learned through careful study that the average individual can move 30ft in a single round and double that speed if running during the same duration of time. Of course various factors discussed in CHAPTER 4 - FEATS & FLAWS could alter this measurement.

Combat is done in a couple parts. A player can make 3 actions in normal combat; first they can move, second they can attack, and third they can use some item or "additional action" that is not movement or attacking. These actions can be done in any order, but only 1 attack can be formed in a round as 6 seconds is too short to attack, and attack again. As stated with movement some Feats and Flaws of an individual may alter these results slightly.

When attacking another individual or SCP it is good to keep in mind your specific strengths and weaknesses. For example someone classified with low "Might" would not be effective in melee combat, while someone with High Agility would be dangerous at a range.

MELEE ATTACKS

When attacking something with your bare hands, a club, sword, or other designated 'melee' weapon, your might is what you would need to focus on. When performing a melee attack you will roll 1D20 (plus any modifiers) and try to beat your Might value. If you succeed you may roll the dice to determine damage, generally in unarmed combat this is 1D4. Once you roll damage, subtract the targets AV (Armor Value) and deal the remaining value to their Health. The GM will roll to see where the attack hits on the target's body unless declared. If a specific target is called add the appropriate modifier to your attack roll: -1 for Body, -2 for a leg, -3 for an arm, -4 for the head. This represents the difficulty of hitting a specific target.

Date: 25/10/██████

Document security clearance level: Class C

Level 0 ☐   Level 1 ☒   Level 2 ☐   Level 3 ☐   Level 4 ☐

RANGED ATTACKS

When attacking something with thrown weapon, bow, gun, or other form of ranged projectile, your agility is what you would need to focus on. When performing a ranged attack you will roll 1D20 (plus any modifiers) and try to beat your Agility value. If you succeed you may roll the dice to determine damage, which is determined by the weapon's damage value. Once you roll damage, subtract the targets AV (Armor Value) and deal the remaining value to their Health. The GM will roll to see where the attack hits on the target's body unless declared. If a specific target is called add the appropriate modifier to your attack roll: -1 for Body, -3 for a leg, -4 for an arm, -5 for the head. This represents the difficulty of hitting a specific target.

AOE & EXPLOSIVE ATTACKS

When attacking something with an explosive or AOE weapon than they target generally has a chance to avoid some of the damage. When you've been successfully hit with an AOE weapon or explosion, roll 1D20. If you roll higher than your Agility, you only take half the damage of the explosive and roll out of it's range by 5ft.

SANITY & SANITY LOSS

While being physically injured is a bad situation to be in, losing your mind can be much worse. As Sanity is much harder to heal and much easier to destroy, it is key that you try to protect your Sanity while within the Foundation. Losing your mind due to SCP or work strain could result in your immediate reclassification to Class D or Class E personnel as circumstance dictates.

Sanity is lost when the mind is subjected to trauma, grotesque experiences, or direct influence from SCP. In most cases this will not be a problem working at the Foundation as we take all security measures and all personnel should feel safe in all facility areas. In the case of a breach of security this section will prove invaluable to have in memory.

SANITY LOSS DUE TO TRAUMA

Certain things in the foundation are just too much for the human mind to bear. As such these things can cause 'passive' damage to your mind and sanity. If experiencing Traumatic or terrific events like a dead body or someone bleeding to death 1D20 should be rolled against your smarts to prevent sanity loss. In these cases the GM would deal sanity damage according to the situation. Examples like the dead body or dying person would probably present 1D4 Sanity damage; while a mutilated corpse, someone being eaten, or a specifically horrifying SCP would cause the player to get a -1 to -5 on their roll with a Sanity damage roll of 1D6 to 2D8.

Date: 25/10/

Document security clearance level: Class C

Level 0 ☐ Level 1 ☒ Level 2 ☐ Level 3 ☐ Level 4 ☐

SANITY LOSS DUE TO FEAR

Certain things will cause you to be afraid. While this in itself does not cause you to take Sanity damage, being too afraid all at once could cause a damaging response in the mind. When moving up the fear track if you move 3 or more up the track within a single combat, or a 5min interval outside of combat; your character will suffer from 2D4 Sanity damage due to the overwhelming fear of the situation.

SANITY DAMAGE ATTACKS

Certain entities in the Foundation will attack and possibly try to feed off the essence of the mind, and as such attacks against your sanity are bound to happen. These entities will have a designated "Damage" value which they can inflict on the mind as well as a "CL" or "Challenge Level" to represent how dangerous their threat is. When the SCP rolls it's Smarts to attack the mind of a target, the target then rolls their Smarts - the CL of the SCP. If they pass they resist the damage and nothing happens. Should the SCP win however than their target (most likely you) will take the full brunt of their damage roll to your Sanity.

RUNNING OUT OF HEALTH OR SANITY

While fighting for your life you may find that you or someone with you has succumb to too much mental or physical trauma and has been 'defeated' for lack of a better more general term. This might not be the end for them however, as this section will go into detail about what to do when someone hits 0 Health or 0 Sanity.

RUNNING OUT OF HEALTH

If a personnel's Health reaches a value of 0, they will be rendered unconscious. Unable to defend themselves, but unable to fight back either. While in this state if they remain at 0 Health without taking any damage or any other trauma for 10 minutes they will wake up with 1 Health. If the personnel is below 0 Health, but above -10 Health they are bleeding out, but alive. They can be stabilized and brought to 0 Health, however a successful Experience check is needed to do so, and a full round. This can only be attempted once on a victim whether successful or not. If unsuccessful or not attempted, than the victim will lose 1 Health every round or 6 seconds until they hit -10 Health. At -10 Health they are dead, and while it hurts us to lose someone, even the Foundation cannot raise the dead. Well except for **[REDACTED]** but that is ill advised.

RUNNING OUT OF SANITY

If a personnel's Sanity reaches a value of 0, they will be rendered paralyzed. They will only be able to babble on the ground, if they can vocalize at all. While in this state the victim is

Date: 25/10/███████

Document security clearance level: Class C

Level 0 ☐   Level 1 ☒   Level 2 ☐   Level 3 ☐   Level 4 ☐

considered unstable. As such they will need time to calm down and recover. When at or below 0 Sanity, but above -10 Sanity, the victim can recover by taking a rest of 10min * (number below 0 Sanity). This means a victim at -5 Sanity would take 10*5 = 50 minutes to recover. After recovering they go up to 1 Sanity. If a victim drops to -10 Sanity they lose their minds entirely and go Insane. Their character card hen goes into the hands of the GM to do with as the universe wishes. We recommend staying as far away from the insane as possible, especially after **[REDACTED]** on **[REDACTED]**.

FEAR, STRAIN, & STRESS

Working in the Foundation can be a stressful, and strenuous thing; as such we wish to convey with you the dangers of putting too much stress, strain, or fear on yourself. A personnel Psycho Analysis Sheet has a section near the top for tracking these three in a "track" style method. Management will want to take note and evaluate if these values get too high.

FEAR

Fear is a simple response to something scary. Generally it causes no trouble to be a little afraid, and in fact it is sometimes expected especially around certain specimens. The problems occur when the fear track becomes higher than 3, showing a significant amount of fear on an individual. Fear is gained through situations where something would cause fear. An Experience roll is made to prevent this cause of fear from affecting you. If you fail you move a number up the fear track equal to the level of fear caused by the object or creature. Other than getting Sanity loss from a 3+ fear jump, simply moving up the fear track can cause negative effects.

At 3 Fear the victim will start to shake and get -1 on rolls to perform tasks until below 3 Fear.

At 4 Fear the victim will try to defend themselves and hide from the object causing them Fear.

At 5 Fear the victim will fall unconscious for 5 minutes.

Fear is very easily stemmed through calming exercise, relaxing words, quiet environments, and some rest. Fear is removed at 1 point 5 minutes spent relaxing. If the area is a "calming situation" then it only takes 2 minutes per 1 point.

STRESS

Stress similar to fear causes effect on the mind. However, unlike Fear, Stress is caused by overworking the mind and causing it to burn out. As such things like failing Experience or Smarts rolls in a tough situation, or getting a 1 on them, will gain you 1 point of Stress. Stress starts having effects at 3 or higher, similar to fear, and can be removed with the same methods as fear. The effects for levels of stress are listed as follows.

Date: 25/10/█████

Document security clearance level: Class C

Level 0 ☐   Level 1 ☒   Level 2 ☐   Level 3 ☐   Level 4 ☐

At 3 Stress the victim will start to shake and get -1 on rolls to perform tasks until below 3 Stress.

At 4 Stress the victim will stop trying tasks involving mental effort and cannot make Smarts or Experience checks of any kind unless in jeopardy; and even then they get -5 to those rolls.

At 5 Stress the victim will simply give up. They won't defend themselves, and will collapse to the ground exhausted. They are forced to start recuperating as soon as this happens, but cannot 'recover' until back down to 0 Stress.

Stress is very easily stemmed through calming exercise, relaxing words, quiet environments, and some rest. Stress is removed at 1 point 5 minutes spent relaxing. If the area is a "calming situation" then it only takes 2 minutes per 1 point.

STRAIN

Strain is a complex reaction of your muscles from overworking them, or pushing them past their limits. When performing a task that is above your capabilities physically, you may do so for 1 strain for 6 seconds of the task. When rolling a 1 on Might or Agility checks (other than when attacking), you move one up the Strain track for pulling something. Strain can be annoying, but does not cause lasting effect until it becomes 3 or greater.

At 3 Strain the victim will start having muscle lock ups and get -1 on rolls to perform tasks until below 3 Strain.

At 4 Strain the victim will be unable to perform tasks involving Might or Agility, besides to defend themselves in combat. Even then these rolls are at -5.

At 5 Strain the victim falls to the ground exhausted and falls unconscious.

Strain requires sleep, relaxation, and massage to recover. Just laying down and sleeping will take 10 min per 1 point recovered. If massaged or given a heat / cold aid, the recovery is sped up to 5 min per 1 point.

KARMA & CURSE

While studying "karma" and 'curses' has yielded little results in terms of measurements, we are in fact able to validate the existence of them in terms of 'good luck' and 'bad luck'. Personnel stated to have high "Karma" are told to have very good luck in situations where luck would be the only useful tool they would have. Similarly, individuals with high 'Curse' would have equally bad luck in situations where luck was the only factor.

As far as we know the only true influences on Karma and Curse are genetics (represented in feats and flaws), and through the influence of the paranormal. Some examples of ways to get each are:

Document security clearance level: Class C

Level 0 ☐   Level 1 ☒   Level 2 ☐   Level 3 ☐   Level 4 ☐

Karma and curses can be gained through influence of certain SCP, other personnel affected by SCP, other personnel with genetically high Karma or Curse, or through the influence of the GM as rewards or punishment for Role Play. The GM will always have final say when giving Karma or Curse, and should try to balance them out, while keeping both somewhat rare.

KARMA

Karma is the measure of good luck your character currently has. This is not just regular good luck, this is "How was that even possible" level of good luck. If a player with Karma fails an important roll, or dies, they can use a point of karma to re-roll the failed roll; or to re-enter their death count at -5 Health or -5 Sanity. Karma is extremely rare and should be used sparingly, as the only attainable ways to get it are to have been brought to the foundation with it (character creation), or through acts of heroic sacrifice deemed worthy by above (The GM). The least likely way to attain it is through an SCP.

CURSE

Curse as the opposite of Karma is the amount of Bad Luck a character currently has. This is not just regular bad luck either, it is "How could this possibly go wrong" level of bad luck. If a player passes a an 'important roll' the GM may use a bad luck point to have them fail that roll instead. If they are stabilized while dying or going insane the GM could also spend a point to reopen the wound or bring back the insanity. Curse is very dangerous and unpredictable because it follows Murphy's Law. In summary "Anything that can go wrong will." Curse is gained through horrible acts, wasting Karma, or interacting with certain cursed SCP objects and specimens.

OTHER SKILL CHECKS

REGULAR (UNCONTESTED)

Skill checks can be made for most situations. When a skill check is needed simply tell the player to roll a 1D20 for the required stat, add a positive or negative to their roll from challenge or circumstance, then take the result. If it is higher than their value for that stat than they succeed, otherwise they fail. Generally a player will get an overwhelming success on a 20 in which they should be rewarded with some unlikely benefit; other times they will get critical failures on a 1, in which case they should have a unlikely bad outcome happen. The same method is used when making an uncontested save using a stat.

CONTESTED SKILL

When doing a contested roll, each player rolls as above for their stat. If both succeed the roll goes again. If no victor is found in 3 rolls than the defender is considered the winner of the contest. A challenge modifier can be added each additional roll to the player with the lower stat. This is generally a -1 per additional roll, or -X where X is their difference in stat value.

SCP

Secure. Contain. Protect.

Date: 25/10/██████

Document security clearance level: Class D

Level 0 ☒   Level 1 ☐   Level 2 ☐   Level 3 ☐   Level 4 ☐

CHAPTER 8 - THE FOUNDATION

**Mankind in its present state has been around for a
quarter of a million years, yet only the last 4,000 have
been of any significance.**

So, what did we do for nearly 250,000 years? We huddled
in caves and around small fires, fearful of the things
that we didn't understand. It was more than explaining
why the sun came up, it was the mystery of enormous birds
with heads of men and rocks that came to life. So we
called them 'gods' and 'demons', begged them to spare us,
and prayed for salvation.

In time, their numbers dwindled and ours rose. The world
began to make more sense when there were fewer things to
fear, yet the unexplained can never truly go away, as if
the universe demands the absurd and impossible.

Mankind must not go back to hiding in fear. No one else
will protect us, and we must stand up for ourselves.

While the rest of mankind dwells in the light, we must
stand in the darkness to fight it, contain it, and shield
it from the eyes of the public, so that others may live
in a sane and normal world.

We secure. We contain. We protect.

— The Administrator

Date: 25/10/▉▉▉▉▉

Document security clearance level: Class C

Level 0 ☐ Level 1 ☒ Level 2 ☐ Level 3 ☐ Level 4 ☐

MISSION STATEMENT

Operating clandestine and worldwide, the Foundation operates beyond jurisdiction, empowered and entrusted by every major national government with the task of containing anomalous objects, entities, and phenomena. These anomalies pose a significant threat to global security by threatening either physical or psychological harm.

The Foundation operates to maintain normalcy, so that the worldwide civilian population can live and go on with their daily lives without fear, mistrust, or doubt in their personal beliefs, and to maintain human independence from extraterrestrial, extradimensional, and other extranormal influence.

Our mission is three-fold:

SECURE

The Foundation secures anomalies with the goal of preventing them from falling into the hands of civilian or rival agencies, through extensive observation and surveillance and by acting to intercept such anomalies at the earliest opportunity.

CONTAIN

The Foundation contains anomalies with the goal of preventing their influence or effects from spreading, by either relocating, concealing, or dismantling such anomalies or by suppressing or preventing public dissemination of knowledge thereof.

PROTECT

The Foundation protects humanity from the effects of such anomalies as well as the anomalies themselves until such time that they are either fully understood or new theories of science can be devised based on their properties and behavior. The Foundation may also neutralize or destroy anomalies as an option of last resort, if they are determined to be too dangerous to be contained.

Date: 25/10/ ▉▉▉▉▉▉

Document security clearance level: Class C

Level 0 ☐   Level 1 ☒   Level 2 ☐   Level 3 ☐   Level 4 ☐

FOUNDATION OPERATIONS

Foundation covert and clandestine operations are undertaken across the globe in pursuit of our primary missions.

SPECIAL CONTAINMENT PROCEDURES

The Foundation maintains an extensive database of information regarding anomalies requiring Special Containment Procedures, commonly referred to as "SCPs". The primary Foundation database contains summaries of such anomalies and emergency procedures for maintaining or re-establishing safe containment in the case of a containment breach or other event.

Anomalies may take many forms, be it an object, an entity, a location, or a free-standing phenomenon. These anomalies are categorized into one of several Object Classes and are either contained at one of the Foundation's myriad Secure Facilities or contained on-site if relocation is deemed unfeasible.

OPERATION SECURITY

The Foundation operates with the utmost secrecy. All Foundation personnel must observe the Security Clearance Levels as well as need-to-know and compartmentalization of information. Personnel found in violation of Foundation security protocols will be identified, detained, and subject to disciplinary action.

RIVAL AGENCIES AND GROUPS OF INTEREST

The Foundation is not the only organization with knowledge of and capability to interact with or utilize anomalies. While some of these Groups of Interest have similar goals and may cooperate with us on issues of global security, many more are opportunistic and profit-oriented, seeking to adapt or use anomalies to their own ends. Foundation personnel are instructed to treat individuals from such groups with suspicion at all times, and collaboration with such groups without the explicit prior consent of Foundation leadership will be cause for termination or other disciplinary action.

SCP INFORMATION

While the Foundation is very well regarded for it's study and findings on SCP Anomalies within our walls, this information is never allowed to leave the facility. As such any SCP files related to this Rulebook can be found at our secret external site at **www.sipcogames.ca/scpbreakout** or more information on the foundations external site at www.scp-wiki.net.

Date: 25/10/██████

Document security clearance level: Class C

Level 0 ☐   Level 1 ☒   Level 2 ☐   Level 3 ☐   Level 4 ☐

SCP PRIMARY CLASSES

These are the most common Object Classes used in SCP articles, and make up the bulk of the objects.

Safe

Safe-class SCPs are anomalies that are easily and safely contained. This is often due to the fact that the Foundation has researched the SCP well enough that containment does not require significant resources or that the anomalies require a specific and conscious activation or trigger. Classifying an SCP as Safe, however, does not mean that handling or activating it does not pose a threat.

Euclid

Euclid-class SCPs are anomalies that require more resources to contain completely or where containment isn't always reliable. Usually this is because the SCP is insufficiently understood or inherently unpredictable. Euclid is the Object Class with the greatest scope, and it's usually a safe bet that an SCP will be this class if it doesn't easily fall into any of the other standard Object Classes.

As a note, any SCP that's autonomous, sentient and/or sapient is generally classified as Euclid, due to the inherent unpredictability of an object that can act or think on its own.

Keter

Keter-class SCPs are anomalies that are exceedingly difficult to contain consistently or reliably, with containment procedures often being extensive and complex. The Foundation often can't contain these SCPs well due to not having a solid understanding of the anomaly, or lacking the technology to properly contain or counter it. A Keter SCP does not mean the SCP is dangerous, just that it is simply very difficult or costly to contain.

Thaumiel

Thaumiel-class SCPs are anomalies that the Foundation uses to contain or counteract other SCPs or anomalous phenomena. Even the mere existence of Thaumiel-class objects is classified at the highest levels of the Foundation and their locations, functions, and current status are known to few Foundation personnel outside of the O5 Council.

Neutralized

Neutralized SCPs are anomalies that are no longer anomalous, either through having been intentionally or accidentally destroyed, or disabled.

Secure. Contain. Protect.

Date: 25/10/████████

Document security clearance level: Class C

Level 0 ☐   Level 1 ☒   Level 2 ☐   Level 3 ☐   Level 4 ☐

SCP OBJECT CLASS INFORMATION

The Locked Box Test

The Locked Box Test is an informal guideline used to determine an object's most appropriate Object Class. It goes like this:

- If you lock it in a box, leave it alone, and nothing bad will happen, then it's probably **Safe**.
- If you lock it in a box, leave it alone, and you're not entirely sure what will happen, then it's probably **Euclid**.
- If you lock it in a box, leave it alone, and it easily escapes, then it's probably **Keter**.
- If it *is* the box, then it's probably **Thaumiel**.

Note that as a special consideration, something that is autonomous, alive, and/or sapient is almost always *at least* Euclid-class. That is, if you lock a living thing in a box and forget about it, it will eventually suffocate or starve to death, and that's not a good outcome. Something that is intelligent could also end up being smart enough to outwit its containment procedures and/or stop cooperating with the Foundation's attempts to contain it, making it more dangerous than it otherwise might be.

Danger and Object Class

Danger does not really affect an SCP's Object Class. As has been reiterated several times above this, an item's Object Class is more based on the difficulty of containment rather than the danger it otherwise poses. For example, a button that can destroy the entire universe when it's pressed would be safe, whereas a cat who randomly switches places with another cat anywhere on earth would be considered Keter.

Secure. Contain. Protect.

Date: 25/10/▮▮▮▮▮

Document security clearance level: Class A

Level 0 ☐   Level 1 ☐   Level 2 ☐   Level 3 ☐   Level 4 ☒

CHAPTER 9 - EXAMPLE STARTING SCENARIO

In SCP: Breakout the general starting scenario involves a group of Class D inmates (The Players), and possibly one Class C Researcher (Most Experienced Player) must escape a facility in crisis. In this scenario (and in fact most scenarios in SCP: Breakout), there will be a Breach of security or catastrophic failure in the containment of a single SCP, or a whole facility.

In our scenario we have a whole facility being breached, and as Class D and Class C personnel their safety was not "mandatory" and they have been left behind. The goal will be to exit the facility safely, and the GM can build their facility in any way they like,in our case we will do a small outliers facility with 2 levels of security blockades.

THE SETUP

First you need to have the players build their Class D (and optionally one Class C Researcher) using the character creation rules with the Normal Difficulty amount of skill pints they can move.

Next as the GM you need to lay out a facility with 2 stages. Make a map with 6 squarish rooms and many hallways ending at an exit gate, than do that again starting from the first exit gate leading to another exit gate. Make the facility maze like as generally facilities are meant to be difficult to navigate and leave. These gates will be designated Gate A (inner gate) and Gate B (outer gate). Gate A will require Class C security to open, while gate A will require Class A security.

Next place a Class C, Class B, and Class A security card randomly in the map for the players to find.

Now use your preferred method to randomize your SCP (or choose your favorites) and place one in each of the 6 rooms. If possible have the players start in the furthest apart room behind Gate A with an SCP that isn't super lethal or strong. Possibly even a helpful one.

Every room with an SCP should also contain either a computer terminal or papers with information about the SCP in that room. This will allow players to learn and figure ways out, even if the SCP is nowhere near their containment room anymore.

Hallways should have Tesla Traps or traps of your own design in them, we recommend about 4 of these traps. You can also add more Class C security doors in the facility to make it a little harder if you like.

THE STORY

Your Class D personnel have been taken into the chamber of an SCP to do some cleaning / testing with it. Your Class C Researcher (Player or not) is outside the chamber taking notes. Suddenly during the rutine the facility goes dark; the containment unit opens, and the SCP (if hostile) breaks out as screams are heard throughout the facility.

Date: 25/10/████████

Document security clearance level: Class C

Level 0 ☐   Level 1 ☑   Level 2 ☐   Level 3 ☐   Level 4 ☐

If the researcher is a player they will have the notes of this SCP, if not then the researcher will also be murdered by an SCP in the facility and drop the notes with their body. From here the backup power kicks in leaving little more than emergency lights on and door manual controls working. The only scanners available are for the Gates A and B that are on their own generators in case of such a failure.

THE GAMEPLAY

In this scenario gameplay is very simple, and the goal is escape. The players will have to fend off SCP in the facility as we will not use other human security officers in this scenario, but you could add them to your own using the stats in the profession chapter and creating a guard template for your facility.

The players will work together to try and escape by navigating hallways and traps. Meanwhile the GM should constantly be having a mental note (or physical notes and rolls) of where their SCP are roaming the facility. The players will not know the whole facility is on lockdown and the SCP are out unless there is a Researcher present among the players.

EVENTS

Events that will happen in your game include:

Running into a Tesla Trap

This event should only happen if the players did not check the hallway, haven't run into one before, or did check the hallway and failed their Agility check to spot it. A Tesla Trap shoots electricity at the first thing to pass through it dealing 8D8 Damage and stunning the victim. It makes a noise before it fires, and encompasses the whole width of the hallway, meaning it has to be passed through or a new route must be found.

If triggered by accident the victim hears a sound and can make a Agility save to take half damage and dive through the Tesla Trap, if they knew the trap was there and attempted to run through it it only deals 50% damage if they fail, and 0% damage if they pass the test. This trap can be used against SCP as well.

Getting hit by (and taking damage from) a Tesla Trap will have the player take a Vitality save to avoid falling unconscious after passing through. If they fail the test they are unconscious for 5 min, otherwise they are considered fine.

Running into a SCP Room

If the room has an SCP in it, use the "Running into an SCP" event first.

If there is no SCP in the room, make sure to leave a few things in the chamber like Scientist clothes, maybe a few tazers or batons, etc. Don't make this every room, but some.

Date: 25/10/████

Document security clearance level: Class C

Level 0 ☐   Level 1 ☒   Level 2 ☐   Level 3 ☐   Level 4 ☐

In addition to any little tidbits in the room, either a desk or a body should have the SCP notes for the SCP designated to that SCP. You should reveal things about the SCP like notes, personality, strengths, weaknesses, and effects. DO NOT reveal their stats however, those are for the players to find out in combat.

Running into an SCP

Running into an SCP can be a blessing, but in most cases it is the worst luck ever. When running into an SCP that is neutral or friendly, follow their scenario accordingly. RP it out with the players.

If the SCP is Hostile or becomes hostile start combat with the players immediately. Most SCP that go Hostile will attempt to attack without warning. Use their SCP sheet to determine their attacks, patterns, and special effects.

Never reveal anythign about an SCP including it's number, unless the players have the SCP information notes from it's room, or the Researcher has a feat allowing them to know that SCP.

Finding a Locked Room or Gate

Your players will inevitably come accross gates or rooms with keycard security scanners. If the players do not have the correct keycard simply explain they see a scanner lock on the door. If they have a keycard below the access needed, the scanner will beep red. If the keycard is at or above the access needed than the scanner will beep green and open the locked door.

A computer wiz or hacker can attempt to unlock these scanners with a negative equal to it's security level (C=-2, B=-4, A=-6, O=-10). If they fail the security door should break and become inaccessible (unless it's a gate, in which case it just cannot be attempted again without failure resulting in the gate being forever sealed).

Scenario Endings / Outcomes

This can very greatly on the number of SCP that are rolled and put into the Facility you have built, but the most common endings would be:

1) They do not escape. The Facility is purged and re-contained and the Players are killed in the process.

2) They escape the facility. If not in Class C researcher outfits with badges, the Class D will be exterminated as per protocol in case of contamination. Any dressed the the researcher outfits or with higher security badges in non Class D clothing can attempt to escape via Smarts or Influence.

3) A particular SCP or Player who's Class E escapes as above relasing the SCP's effects into society with detrimental effect.

CHAPTER 10 - CHARACTER SHEETS & RESOURCES

ACKNOWLEDGEMENTS

The Foundation and SCP are a community creation with lore from many different authors. As such any references to SCP's or the Foundation are to be held under Creative Commons Agreement **CC-BY-SA 3.0** as requested on **http://www.scp-wiki.net**

Any work on the VGS System or SCP: Breakout RPG resources not related to the SCP Foundation wiki or SCP's specifically, are Copyright of Sipco Games.

In short you are free to copy and use anything that is used in this book that is related to the Foundation and SCP with credit given to SCP: Breakout and the SCP Wiki; but use of the VGS system for any other commercial work is not allowed without express written consent from Adam Sippel, Owner Sipco Games.

WHERE ARE THE SCP FILES?

In order to make SCP's easier to use and understand they will be free to view, use, and download from our site at **www.sipcogames.ca/scpbreakout**. We will release credited books for these SCP to be purchased as well, but as all credit for SCP creation belongs to their respective authors we wish to offer all of the information for free and credit all authors respectively.

CHARACTER SHEETS

Otherwise referred to as Psycho Analysis Sheets, these sheets are available on the next couple pages to tear out, photocopy, or otherwise use as character sheets for your players. The alternative is to download and print off copies from our website at **www.sipcogames.ca/scpbreakout.**

SCP

Secure. Contain. Protect

PSYCHO ANALYSIS SHEET - 1

FEAR: OOOOO KARMA: OOOOO

STRAIN: OOOOO CURSE: OOOOO

STRESS: OOOOO

	Current	Temp
MIGHT		
AGILITY		
VITALITY		
SMARTS		
EXPERIENCE		
INFLUENCE		

PLAYER: _____

GM: _____

HEIGHT: _____

WEIGHT: _____

HAIR: _____

EYES: _____

PERSONALITY: _____

LIKES: _____

DISLIKES: _____

POSITION

CLASS

HEAD

BODY

R. ARM

L. ARM

R. LEG

L. LEG

SANITY

/

HEALTH

/

ARMOR

/

FEATS

FLAWS

Secure. Contain. Protect

PSYCHO ANALYSIS SHEET - 2

Weapon:	Damage:	Weight:	Type:
Special Functions:			

Weapon:	Damage:	Weight:	Type:
Special Functions:			

Weapon:	Damage:	Weight:	Type:
Special Functions:			

GEAR & EQUIPMENT   WEIGHT CURRENT: [   ]   MAX WEIGHT: [   ]

lbs.	GEAR	lbs.	GEAR
____	_____	____	_____
____	_____	____	_____
____	_____	____	_____
____	_____	____	_____
____	_____	____	_____
____	_____	____	_____
____	_____	____	_____
____	_____	____	_____
____	_____	____	_____
____	_____	____	_____
____	_____	____	_____
____	_____	____	_____
____	_____	____	_____
____	_____	____	_____
____	_____	____	_____
____	_____	____	_____
____	_____	____	_____

Date: 25/10/▮▮▮▮

Document security clearance level: Class D

Level 0 ☒   Level 1 ☐   Level 2 ☐   Level 3 ☐   Level 4 ☐

THANK YOU!

Thank you in your support of our RPG game development! We love to make all the tabletop games that are hopefully enjoyed by many! While this game is very open ended compared to most we've made, the large community around SCP and the seemingly endless amount of content we can add to this game is incredible. We will be slowly adding SCP guides and resources online for free as well as periodically releasing SCP Information books for purchase as we are able. We cannot wait to see what everyone does with SCP: Breakout, and we hope you enjoy.

From Everyone Here
at Sipco Games!
THANK YOU AND ENJOY!

CPSIA information can be obtained
at www.ICGtesting.com
Printed in the USA
LVHW060824040121
674959LV00004BA/203